To Violet,
thank you
for being
amazing and
such an inspiration!
Never stop being
incredible!
            - Zach

HUNGERS AS OLD
AS THIS LAND

"With *Hungers as Old as This Land*, Zach Rosenberg continues to carve a niche as a leading voice in Jewish horror. And with good reason! Where horror can often fall back on tropes related to fear of the 'other,' Zach's sharp, incisive prose instead elevates and spotlights the differences that connect us as human beings, setting us in conflict with forces of conformity, prejudice, and greed— the true terrors of existence in America from throughout its history."

—Patrick Barb, author of *Pre-Approved for Haunting and Other Stories*

"I go to horror westerns for camp, good fun, and plenty of gore, all three of which this novella by Zach Rosenberg had in spades. *Hungers as Old as This Land* freshens up the western trope with two tough-as-nails female leads in Esther Foxman and Siobhan O'Clery. Though the going isn't always easy for them, they back down from no one, and always have each other's back. I particularly enjoyed the Jewish culture and horror woven throughout (something I haven't seen before in a Western)—ending with a bang in the mountains beyond Grey Bluffs. *Hungers* packs plenty of action, humor, and heart. If you like horror westerns you'll dig this one."

—Caleb Stephens, author of *Only a Heart*

"Esther and Siobhan are the perfect leads for this whirlwind read featuring creepy creatures and a delightfully hateable antagonist. *Hungers As Old As This Land* should be put at the top of your TBR list."

—Stephanie Rabig, author of *On Stolen Land*

"Zach Rosenberg's *Hungers as Old as This Land* left me shaken but satisfied. Applying the same level of craft to the explosive gun battles and fist fights as he does to the tender moments between two frontier women; Zach writes with style and heart. And this horror western doesn't hesitate to bleed that heart. Lurking under the surface is a sculpted shadow of dread so lurid, I was worried I might not make it back to the light. Trust Zach Rosenberg to skillfully guide you through these dark hollows, just make sure you pack extra provisions (and extra bullets)."

—Alan Lastufka, author of *Face the Night*

"*Hungers* delivers darkness without extinguishing light, cauterizing the wounds it inflicts."

—Coy Hall, author of *The Hangman Feeds the Jackal* and *Grimoire of the Four Imposters*

"Rosenberg's writing is finessed and sharp, his characters vibrant and hard-boiled...there's danger and love on every page, as well as a brilliant defiance from the oppressed."

—Aiden Merchant, author of *Sickness is in Season* and *Crossing Red*

"Take a Western with elements of folk horror, throw in love and betrayal and promises broken and you get *Hungers as Old as This Land*. A story layered with subtle darkness and irresistible mystery reveals Zachary Rosenberg as a skilled storyteller and spinner of yarns—a writer to take notice of."

—Stephanie Ellis, author of *The Five Turns of the Wheel*, *Paused*, and *Reborn*

"In Rosenberg's *Hungers as Old as the Land* we get a tale filled with vengeance, greed and a really intriguing folklore aspect that'll have you wishing to learn more! This novella races along to a horrifying finale that'll have readers smiling!"

—Steve Stred, Splatterpunk-Nominated author of
Mastodon and *Churn the Soil*

HUNGERS AS OLD AS THIS LAND

by Zachary Rosenberg

Brigids Gate PRESS™

Edited by Kenneth W. Cain

Proofread and formatted by Stephanie Ellis
Cover illustration and design by Kealan Patrick Burke

First Edition: May 2023
ISBN (paperback): 9781957537467
ISBN (ebook): 9781957537450
Library of Congress Control Number: 2023932788

BRIGIDS GATE PRESS

Bucyrus, Kansas

www.brigidsgatepress.com

Printed in the United States of America

For my parents, Debbie and Nathan, and my sister Julia, who never stopped helping me to dream.

To all my author friends, past and present, who have helped me shape every bizarre thought into something legible. All of us are just getting started.

Content warnings are provided at the end of this book

CHAPTER ONE

The battlefield breathed death. He could smell it, almost taste it. It had been ten straight hours of musket fire and cannons roaring all throughout Antietam. After all he had seen, Cyril Redstone was beginning to believe there were no rules to warfare.

Clad in a uniform that might have been pristine blue—if not for mingling stains of mud, ash and human blood—Cyril crouched down in the trench with an eye set upon Jimmy Franks. Only two days ago, Jimmy had been talking and laughing around the campfires with the rest of their brigade. Even now, Jimmy's mouth was still open, but no laughter emanated from it. There was no more twinkle in his eyes, having lost both thanks to a pair of rebel sharpshooters. All around them, the blood and brains of men too impatient and too foolish to know how to survive mingled with the wet earth.

Cyril caught himself wondering who the dead men had been just hours ago, what dreams they might have possessed. He concentrated hard on the field, desperate to see a way out. A cannon exploded somewhere in the distance, ripping him from his careful contemplation.

He instinctively pressed his back against the trench, ignoring how the cold mud seeped through to his skin. He could worry about catching ill later. His primary concern was to stay alive. The hard wood of the musket felt strange in his hands. Yet it comforted him, a constant reminder that he still had a weapon with which to fight.

"Who's winnin' up there, Foxman?" Cyril called to the nearest soldier, raising his voice to be heard above the din even though the man was close enough to touch. Foxman was slightly younger than he, his black hair the same shade as the dark gun smoke drifting above them. His smooth features and gentle hazel eyes made him look strangely unsuited for the battlefield he now resided upon. One of his hands clutched a six-pointed star that hung at his throat.

"Let me just peek my head above the trench and let you know, why don't I, Redstone?" Foxman said back.

Abraham Foxman was a fine soldier, one Cyril counted on to have his back. The light banter was a reminder they were still alive and had kept hold of their wits.

"What're you so scared of? They can only kill us once." Foxman lifted his rifle as he said it, the silent vow of a soldier who did not intend to go quietly.

Cyril flashed his teeth, though there was no humor in his smile. General McClellan had evidently committed fewer than three-quarters of his troops to the engagement. *Lucky how that played out*, Cyril thought.

He looked back to the field, trying to scan for anything that might give him optimism. But all he saw were fields blackened by ash. Men screamed and died; shot full of lead or disemboweled by bayonets and sabers. Trampled underneath horses or torn apart by cannonballs, men in gray and blue alike forsook whatever ambitions they carried with them into Antietam to become the future dinner for carrion birds.

Abraham Foxman turned, finding the impossible bravery somewhere in his soul to peek out over the trench.

He lifted his musket to shoulder level and pulled the trigger, Cyril wincing at the thunderous crack in his ear. Foxman ducked back beside Cyril.

"I damn well hope you hit General Lee so we can wrap this up!"

In response, Foxman methodically reloaded with nimble motions. He came back up, risking danger to fire another shot that reduced the rebel army's forces by one man. "God willing! The Lord's with us today, Cyril."

Other soldiers often derided Abraham Foxman for his faith behind his back. But in Cyril's opinion, any god that might exist was no friend to the men in the trenches. He couldn't have possibly cared less what Foxman believed so long as he could aim, shoot, and drop another bastard rebel grayback.

Cyril took Foxman's place atop the trench. He pointed his gun at a charging man and fired, catching the Confederate in the throat. Before the man had fallen to the earth, Cyril was back in the safety of the trench, holding his hand out to Foxman. "Keep your god and pass me some more lead."

Gunshots cracked overhead while Cyril reloaded, shrieks of the dead and the dying flowing across the field. A bugle sounded, some commanding officer's voice rising over the din with the clearest of orders.

"Crazy bastards mean to have us charge." Cyril grasped the rifle all the tighter as though it might ward off the coming storm.

"Maybe it means we're winning." Foxman's smile was fearless enough for Cyril to envy. He was an idealist, a true believer in the righteousness of the Union cause.

Cyril believed in the payment promised on his enlistment contract. Dead men couldn't spend dollars.

"You watch my back, I'll watch yours. We'll see you get home to your little girl."

The bugle sounded again, delivering clear orders. The men were already pulling themselves up, scrambling over the corpses of comrades and enemies alike, to commit themselves to a charge.

Cyril knew there could be no further delays. Summoning iron to his belly, he scrambled up the muddy side of the trench. Foxman moved with him, the two sliding over the trenches to join a blue tide of advancing soldiers. Cyril kept ahead of Foxman, the burst of musket fire filling his ears.

Then Cyril tripped.

Stumbling down, Cyril sank to his knees and toppled face first into the mud. Trying to push himself back up, he found himself staring into a puddle of cooling blood. He raised his head, a rebel standing close in front of him. The man had his musket up, aiming it at Cyril's face. Time froze for just an instant as Cyril raised his own rifle, but the grayback had him. He heard the gunshot, and a coin-sized hole appeared on the gray-uniformed man's cheek. A spray of brains exploded out the back of his head, the man falling to join the rest of the dead.

"Redstone, Redstone!" Foxman had him, pulling him to his feet.

Cyril shrugged away the man's hand, righting himself and realizing Foxman had just saved his life. Fortune had placed him close by to take that shot.

"Are you alright?" Foxman's voice was tinged with genuine concern.

"Look after yourself," Cyril grunted, realizing he was in Abraham Foxman's debt. Without further words, the two rushed on, joining the charge of Union soldiers. Cyril managed to slow his stride just enough to let Foxman run ahead of him. If the man was so eager to place himself in harm's way in defense of Cyril's life, so be it. Cyril intended to live, to flourish. Those were the only things that mattered to him now; what he hungered for. Concealed behind a shield of stampeding, uniformed bodies, Cyril committed himself to the final charge, roaring as a lion so he might sell the image just a little bit better.

It was the seventeenth of September, 1862.

CHAPTER TWO

Riding high in the saddle with her lover beside her, Esther Scenanki Foxman could feel the touch of the Almighty.

Laughing as Lacey, her chestnut-brown quarter horse, committed herself to another sprint, Esther gripped the reins tighter. "I'll bet ya I make it to the front before ya, Siobhan!" She turned her head to the side to view Siobhan.

Mounted upon her faithful, dappled horse, Padraig, Siobhan O'Clery flashed a pair of white teeth at Esther, hair fluttering behind her. "What're we wagerin', darlin'?" There was a sparkle in Siobhan's eyes as she grasped Padraig's reins. "A kiss from the maiden fair, mayhaps?"

"Siobhan, my dear, I don't need a reward to kiss ya. But in the spirit of competition?" Esther cast a smirk at the other woman, proud of the redness she could induce in those pale, freckled cheeks with just the flutter of her own dark eyes. Undeterred, Siobhan leaned forth in her saddle, too skilled a rider to let minor embarrassment disorient her. "Not flaggin' are you?"

"I'll show ya flaggin' before this is done," Siobhan returned, her fiery spirit roused by the prospect of competition. There was no glimmer of fatigue in her voice, a life of frontier labor leaving both with ample stamina.

"Oh, will ya?" Esther delighted in the chance for some enjoyment, knowing she could not say who would be the victor. The two were on an errand for the settlement of

Grey's Bluffs, dispatched by Esther's father around dawn. First, they were to stop by the mountains, before taking a diversion to the nearest town. The whole affair would take well over a day before they returned home, but both were delighted by time alone together as they fulfilled the needs of their settlement.

"Just watch me!" Siobhan drove her heels into Padraig's side with a wordless shout. The dappled horse trilled out and rushed ahead in full gallop.

Not to be outdone, Esther spurred Lacey onward, the quarter horse soon catching the other equine. The plains were clear, with no use Esther might see for the gun holstered at her side.

Lacey had been an absolute good sport throughout the ride, what with the burden she held upon her back. The horse seemed to be enjoying the ride as much as Esther, getting to stretch her legs and slam her hooves into the dirt as they galloped forth to the mountains ahead.

Esther had performed this same trip dozens of times over the years. As the settlement leader's daughter, such duties were placed on her shoulders. It was expected of her, and she performed her role without complaint. As a result, Grey's Bluffs and the people within prospered well.

Esther snapped the reins like a whip, her laughter mingling with Siobhan's as the wind sweetly stung their faces. She and Siobhan exchanged joyous looks, blue eyes to black. The mountains loomed closer, Esther driving Lacey to a final burst of speed so she might overtake Siobhan. But Siobhan had expected it, conserving Padraig's strength for the last stretch.

The horses cleared the target almost simultaneously, the women slowing them from the run to a tired trot as soil gave way to hard rock.

Esther dismounted Lacey and whispered endearments into a flicking ear. "I think I won that one."

"I beg your pardon, Esther Foxman?" Siobhan was already on the ground, hands on her hips. "Just because ya might be the prettiest lady in all the territory, doesn't mean I'll let you get away with base dishonesty."

Siobhan's father had met Abraham Foxman as a soldier in the Southern Rebellion. Afterwards, he became a minister, an educated man who had passed a love of learning on to his daughter before his death. But Abraham Foxman had made arrangements to care for his old comrade's orphaned child, having recently lost his own wife, believing it would do his daughter well to have a companion. Siobhan's love of books had captivated Esther since the days of their childhood. She had spent hours teaching Siobhan Hebrew, just as Siobhan taught her Latin and Gaelic—four tongues to proclaim their love for one another in. Some in Grey's Bluffs did not fully understand their feelings, but Abraham Foxman accepted it. She and Siobhan had one another, and that was good enough for Esther.

"I ain't tellin' no lies." Esther released the burden from Lacey's back—freshly butchered meat wrapped in a sack. Just what they were here to deliver. Esther's smile briefly faltered as she scanned the mountains, seeing no movement. If Siobhan felt any trepidation, she gave no sign of it.

"We ain't in the territory yet. No reason to fret." Despite her confident tone, Siobhan's hand remained close to the gun at her own side.

"Just worried our friends might be a touch peckish is all." Esther set the sack on the ground. "Damn, but that's heavy. Siobhan, ya wanna help—"

Esther stopped as Siobhan crossed the distance to her and pressed her lips against Esther's. Siobhan kissed her with a soft, tender passion, the intimacy of a woman who had kissed the same lips a thousand times and knew the right way to savor them.

Siobhan shifted back slightly while keeping her forehead pressed to her lover's, as though wishing to savor the feel of Esther's dark skin against hers. "Shalom."

Esther brought her mouth up and eagerly stole another kiss like it was the greatest of treasures. "Shalom yourself. Fine, I'm alright. Ya can kiss me all ya like when we're clear of the Hungers."

Now she did see movement against a mountainside. Something large and swift vanishing along one peak. Esther breathed in and out. Siobhan or no, it was impossible to breathe easy, pact or no pact.

Hauling the sacks of meat, the two walked down the mountain trail, flanked by the great peaks known as the Hungers. Esther breathed slowly, taking one step at a time. For all her confidence before, there was no such thing as a man or woman in Grey's Bluffs who could approach the Hungers without trepidation.

"Think we're bein' watched?" Esther moistened her lips as the cold air whistled by her head. She scanned the mountains, saw shadows moving against the snow. Furtive and so quick that one could have mistaken them for sun-cast shadows.

"Without a doubt." Siobhan's hand twitched near the revolver at her side, something Esther knew was sheer instinct. "Let's get this done and get out quick."

"Yeah, not a step further."

Esther stopped before the winding pass that led further to the mountains, ten strides from the mouth of the old caves. Siobhan froze, and Esther took one step forward, laying down the sacks of meat before unfurling them to reveal heaps of butchered cuts of sheep and cow. Esther stared into the mouth of the cave, darkness greeting her eyes.

"My name is Esther Foxman, daughter of Abraham Foxman, whose pact was signed in blood with those of the Hungers." She spoke the words her father had taught her, the words of the pact with the Hungers clear and strong. She showed neither weakness, nor fear. Such things would only get them killed. "My people are exiles, prospering by the grace of those who've long been here. For our pact and our prosperity, I bring you food to feed you and yours."

Wildlife was plentiful near the Hungers. Those within wanted for little and so demanded nothing substantial. A few sheep every year was enough to keep them sated and to honor the bargain established many years prior. Esther waited a long moment, staring into the darkness. She heard a clicking noise in the cave, akin to sharp knives tapping together. Esther pushed the meat forward, bringing it closer to the maw of the cave. She stopped short from entering the blackness.

"I bid you farewell. There will be more the following cycle." She ended with the same promise she always gave.

Something darted from the mouth of the cave with the speed of a snapping whip. A dark hand seized a cut of raw meat, dripping with blood, and yanked it back into the darkness. Esther heard a wet tearing sound followed by that of flesh being shredded by something sharp. Then that of teeth chomping and rapid chewing.

The growl that followed was guttural, but unmistakably English forced against an unfamiliar tongue. *"Go."*

Esther took the sacks with her, leaving the remainder of the meat upon the ground. She returned to Siobhan's side, offering a quick grin towards the cave, a salute of two fingers at her head. "See ya next time then."

She let herself sag into Siobhan's arms with relief, the two turning with lessened burdens to set back toward the horses. Lacey and Padraig were unharmed, though clearly agitated and delighted to see the two again.

Esther walked up, hand running against her quarter horse's long face as she whispered endearments to her. "Looks like they were good as their word, then."

Scattered about the horses was a collection of gold— thick nuggets plucked from deep within the mountains, some chunks the size of Esther's fist. She began to fill the sacks with relief, calculating how much weight Lacey and Padraig could bear.

"We ride over to town," she said, "get this exchanged, hit the bank, and head home. Then I'm gonna fill a bath, heat it up, and not get outta bed for a few days."

"Speakin' my language," Siobhan mused, brushing her hand to Esther's back as they led their horses from the mountain trail. Esther paused at the sound of something sharp sliding over rock. She looked up at a mountain ledge, seeing a pair of dark shapes hidden in folds of shadows.

"Our honor guard," Esther muttered, feeling the weight of her pistol at her side, hoping she could soon forget the notion of why it was even necessary. Part of the deal entailed ensuring those who delivered tribute made it safely home to Grey's Bluffs. Her father had been insistent this was not negotiable.

"Just like every year. Pretend they ain't there." Siobhan put a hand to Esther's back and urged her on. "Try not to worry. Ya know they won't harm us."

"It ain't us I'm worried about." Esther shuffled forth, trying to banish their guards from her mind.

"We ain't ever had troubles they've needed to intervene in," Siobhan reminded her. Esther recalled the wet sounds of feasting from the caves.

"Just talk to me about somethin' else. Tell me what we'll do when we get back home." She focused solely on her lover, a silent plea in her eyes.

Siobhan brushed a finger to Esther's cheek in response, her voice gentle. "Figure we take that breather before we get to drivin' cattle and seein' about the crops. Ya don't think anyone'll notice? Your daddy won't have any problems?"

"I have the feelin' we'll be just fine." Esther leaned over and stole another kiss, still attempting to forget the shadows, even as she knew they were following close. "Thanks for comin' with, Siobhan O'Clery."

"No place I'd rather be than right with ya, Esther Foxman. Now, c'mon. Longer we delay, more Tobias will worry. You know that boy won't forgive us if we're late to get back."

Chuckling to herself, Esther could not resist seizing the star around her throat and whispering a prayer in Hebrew, of thanks and deliverance. She could feel eyes boring into her back, watching her and Siobhan depart.

Grey's Bluffs was a new settlement, a town not even twenty years old, established by Abraham Foxman and his closest allies some years after the Southern Rebellion. But the Hungers had been waiting when they arrived. The Hungers existed long before Grey's Bluffs and would continue to thrive long after the town was gone. As she walked off with her love at her side, she left the Hungers to their feast, their silent guards trailing unseen after them.

It was the fourteenth of October, 1881.

***

Cyril Redstone did not like when dying men seized his ankles, getting blood all over his boots. He aimed his gun at Jack Roberts, offering a bored shrug to counter the begging in the other man's eyes. After calculating if Jack was worth the bullet, Cyril ended the plea for mercy with a small clench of his finger around the trigger. Whatever Jack had to say was silenced by the bullet through his eye, the man reduced to nothing more than a payment waiting to be collected.

Being paid to wipe out a group of unionizing workers was all in a day's work for the Blackhawks. Men out of the quarry were doubtlessly crouching in their own camps, hunkered down and trying to pretend they didn't hear the distant noises of gunfire. Cyril had sent word to the miners that they had simply intended a meeting on behalf of Bancroft & Hughes Mining and Railroad Conglomerate to discuss acceding to the unionizers' demands, though company owner Gerard Bancroft had intended a more permanent solution when he'd hired the Blackhawks.

The meeting had been on Cyril's terms, with no intention of negotiations. Miners were cattle, beasts of burden. When you had one that proved itself obstinate and dragged others down with it, you didn't waste time negotiating. You thinned the herd and moved on.

Judging by the hoots and victorious jeers from the Blackhawks, in their red and black coats, holstering their pistols and cleaning off their knives, the culling had been effective and hopefully the rest of the cattle would know their place.

"What do we do with the bodies here, Cyril?" Nicky Rackets said. He was a bearded, red-faced, and ill-tempered man who had a fondness for whiskey and violence. This was not so unusual for all thirty of the Blackhawks, a unit of 'problem solvers' who came highly recommended when it came to scaring stubborn workers and townsfolk. They were not a group famous for their brains, most relying on Cyril to do the negotiating, the planning, and the thinking for them.

"Take those fellas down past the mines and chuck 'em into the nearest hole you find." Cyril gave a careless shrug. "When they're missin', it'll say as much as if they find bodies full of lead." Bancroft didn't want evidence that could be traced back to him, even if no other miners were likely to be brave enough to try.

Percival Beard, a squat man with less impressive facial hair than his name might have implied, was wiping a hand over his forehead, stripping down one body to search for valuables.

Cyril removed himself from Jack's corpse, already annoyed enough that the man had gotten blood on his new boots. "Make that disappear." He flicked his revolver at the corpse before he slid the gun back into its holster. "Don't take too long about it."

He'd grown since the Civil War and the nearly twenty years that had followed. He had survived Antietam and Gettysburg, had marched all the way to Appomattox to collect his final payments from the army and to decide his own destiny for himself. He found his calling in the West where the borders of states ended and territories began.

Cyril was a man of America, whether he marched under the Stars and Stripes or ran with his own unit. With a group of veterans, disaffected lawmen, police officers, and those who simply wanted a profit, he had found his little place in the world as a problem solver for men with means. The Blackhawks had killed for the army, killed for local magistrates and mayors, and, in other instances, they had killed union organizers for the rich and powerful.

America was a place where they would never run out of work.

"We head back to Independence after you take care of them corpses, lads!" Cyril raised his voice to be heard by all of them, hearing his own words reverberate across the quarry. "First round at the tavern's on me later!"

He removed a canteen from his side, unscrewed it, and poured tepid water down his throat, already envisioning the bite of good whiskey. Killing was thirsty work.

***

Independence was more city than settlement now. Walled and vast, Independence was a growing titan of industry, thick rails laid across the plains to pave the way to the trading hub. Workers swarmed around, salesmen plying their wares. Women leaned out of saloon windows to wave coquettishly to the passersby.

Cyril had left his horse at the stables, giving his lads permission to see to drink and whatever they wanted as long as they kept the hell raising to a reasonable minimum. It was not uncommon for a Blackhawk to kill a man in a brawl or some disagreement, but Cyril preferred to keep that to the more remote regions of the territories. Doing so below your employer's place of business was both discourteous and unwise.

Cyril walked through the streets, singularly focused until he reached the offices, a gold plate with "Bancroft &

Hughes" decorated the door. The man inside recognized him, nodding him through.

The West was still wild in many ways. Human beings believed they could tame the land, force it to obey their hungers. Men like Gerard Bancroft were giving that their best damned shot, carving away at the wilderness to leave only metal and brick. The office was nothing short of modern and civilized in a way that made Cyril's lip curl internally. He was a man of frontiers and battlefields. The pale and sterile walls disquieted him more than the blood-soaked soil after a killing.

But Bancroft was paying enough to make retirement look mighty promising. His office door was open, revealing a solitary desk occupied by the man himself. Gerard Bancroft was small, with plain features and eyes the steely gray of little coins. His hair was thinning, his body clad in a finely tailored suit. He looked up, the most ordinary fellow that could disappear into a crowd of three while also being able to buy them out a million times over.

"Mr. Redstone." Even his voice was unremarkable.

"Mr. Bancroft." Men like Gerard Bancroft placed great value on proprieties. To most of society, Cyril was not spoken of in polite company. To Bancroft, he was useful as long as proper protocols were followed.

"I trust there is no further talk of unionizing among my workers?"

"Little hard for some of them to talk about anythin' anymore, Mr. Bancroft." Cyril did not need to elaborate.

"Very good." If Bancroft took any pleasure from the news, he did not show it. The death of numerous men were likely just further marks on a ledger for him. He fixed his eyes on Cyril in his dark coat, studying the mercenary. "Wipe that smirk off your face, Cyril. You're in a place of business and I'll ask you to conduct yourself appropriately. But you've performed quick and efficient, just as I expected. You learned well from your time in the Pinkertons."

"And the army," Cyril said with a shrug, scratching his smooth cheek. "If you could get the same value from the Pinks, you would, Mr. Bancroft."

"They do tend to ask some unfortunate questions and charge a little extra for the answers," Bancroft agreed. He was already removing a sheet of paper and lifting a pen to it. "Bring that note to my clerk and the money shall be retrieved for you shortly."

"That's why I like working with you, sir. You pay quick and on time." Cyril grinned enough to show his teeth. "You know how to patch a message for us should you need us next time."

"Sit down, Cyril."

Bancroft was removing a bottle of brandy from his desk, along with two small glasses. This was an unexpected privilege. He lowered himself into the seat without complaint. Bancroft filled both glasses and slid one to Cyril.

He took a drink. It tasted rich, a good burn down his throat. Nothing like the cheap stock he loved most in the saloons, but he drank all the same so as not to offend. "New job you need done?"

"Clearly." Bancroft's little gray eyes narrowed, his hands folding on the table once he set his own glass down.

"Have you discussed it with Mr. Hughes?"

"Kenneth is aware," Bancroft said with an airy wave of his hand. "The railroad is under his purview, but this involves the both of us. Have you heard of a settlement called Grey's Bluffs?"

"I can't say it's sparkin' my recognition." There were a thousand little towns and settlements all over the West. He could hardly be expected to have heard of them all. "You need someone there removed? Another strike?" Cyril made a dismissive gesture. "I think you know we're good for dealing with stubborn workers."

"They do not work for me. Which I confess galls me, because everyone around here is supposed to work for me in some way or another—from the proprietor of the general corner store, to the miners in the quarries, to the women in the brothels. Every coin they make comes back to me in this region. Grey's Bluffs not only defies this natural order; they do not even partake of the scrip I offer."

Cyril chuckled at that, leaning back to cross his feet, turning the empty glass around with his fingers. "Sounds like you're askin' me for a touch of mass murder."

"Your words, not mine."

"Your intentions, my deeds," Cyril returned. "What do I need to know for this here job?"

"Every year, people from Grey's Bluffs come into town at the trading hubs." Bancroft, bless him, recognized when it was time to truly talk shop. "They bring with them gold, freshly mined from the mountains known as the Hungers.

"The town was founded by those whose faith did not quite agree with the city Christian folk. Some of that particular persuasion have indeed set out west. Several have even been quite successful. A Levi Strauss fashioned a new pair of pants I'm told are quite comfortable."

"Well, I'm just about thrilled for our Hebrew friends," Cyril remarked with an apathetic shrug. "I heard about it, killed a few of 'em when I had to, same as anyone else. What makes this special?"

"Grey's Bluffs is located on valuable land. It would be perfect to demolish and run a track through, as well as set up mining rights in the Hungers. You know the mountains? They had something of a reputation. Do you believe in ghost stories, Cyril?" Bancroft chuckled with the nervous confidence of a man who believed enough not to test any of the stories.

That was a surprise to Cyril, who thought Bancroft's only belief to be money. "I've had a fair few folks invoke all manner of dark curses in their hour of dyin'. Can't say I put much stock in that."

"Good." Bancroft regained his composure, speaking deliberately as if trying to convince himself. "Superstition has little place in matters of business. I have tried to speak with the headman of this little village, but he proves irritatingly reticent. We worked out a contract for agricultural rights that does turn a tidy profit, but it is hardly a drop in the proverbial bucket. There are no tribes in the direct area to worry about, save those who occasionally trade with Grey's Bluffs. The town, however, is wealthy. I believe the proprietor has a small trading empire of his own. Unfortunately, Mr. Abraham Foxman has proved rather reluctant to sell anything."

Cyril paused suddenly, freezing as he looked into Bancroft's eyes. "What name did you just say to me?"

"Abraham Foxman. He was a soldier, one who prospered in dried goods for a time until his move west. His late wife was a member of the Muscogee Creek—" Bancroft looked into Cyril's eyes. "You know this man?"

"He saved my life in the war." Cyril's mind went back to that bloody day at Antietam when he had slipped in the mud, when the man in gray had trained that rifle on him. "A damn reb nearly had me. Foxman was the one who put a bullet in him. Saved my life, I'm not too proud to admit I'd not be talkin' to you if not for him. You're askin' me to kill a man who I owe my very breath to."

"I was not aware you two knew one another." Bancroft folded his hands. He was suddenly quite tense, his gaze drifting to the hip where Cyril kept his gun. Cyril wondered if Bancroft feared for his life and it gave him no small enjoyment to intimidate such a wealthy man for even a moment. "Am I to understand you will not take this job?"

Cyril looked into Bancroft's eyes. He let a slow smile stretch over his face, a sudden hunger burning within his gut. "I'm just sayin' for an undertakin' of this emotional importance? It's gonna cost you double. That ain't gonna be a problem, is it?"

"Cyril," Bancroft began with visible relief "your ability to be reasonable is a never-ending source of delight to me."

"Everythin' has a price, Mr. Bancroft. After all, this here's America."

CHAPTER THREE

Esther was beginning to think she couldn't take Siobhan anywhere. She had stopped close to several traders she knew in Independence, exchanging the gold for real money, not the cheap strips of paper that Bancroft enforced on his company towns. She had made Siobhan promise to stay out of trouble. Her lover had responded by blowing a kiss and stalking off.

Esther kept to the open streets. As a lone woman with dark skin carrying a great deal of money, she did not wish to be a target. Her concern was mostly for anyone who might be unlucky enough to try to rob her. Though she could not see the bodyguards that had followed them from the Hungers, Esther knew full well they were nearby.

She already knew where Siobhan was and had every intention of meeting up with her. Esther could feel the eyes on her, her hat tipped down, though not low enough that the dark shade of her skin was not apparent. Like most places in the good United States, territory or official state, segregation was enforced whether it was official or not. Esther's mother's people had been taken from their lands like so many other tribes and nations. Her father's people faced discrimination and distrust as well. Abraham explained its persistence to her, how it had followed their ancestors long after they had been expelled from England, Spain, France, Germany and more.

Such towns and settlements held good white folks to be superior to Blacks, to the Chinese laborers, to the Native peoples, to the Jews. Esther was trusted implicitly by her father, and she knew she had protections beyond what others in her position might have otherwise enjoyed. The way people looked at her, the expressions on their faces were still an eternal reminder of how little she fit in outside of Grey's Bluffs.

The irony was Esther had never truly known her mother's people. Halona Foxman had died when Esther was just a little girl, not long after the war. While Abraham never said anything out loud, he was still the single father of a young Muscogee-born daughter. Doubtless that was a large reason for him trying his luck out west. Though he had passed on the ways of his line to her, raised her in his faith, his knowledge of Halona's ways and traditions had been limited at best.

There were even some Jewish men and women who looked down upon people born to such unions. Esther was proud of her heritage nonetheless, Jewish and Creek alike. She proudly represented her faith with the six-pointed star around her neck, an heirloom from her father's ancestors in Prague nearly two centuries prior.

Her lover was still perhaps the one person she felt wholly at peace with. Siobhan O'Clery, with her fiery red hair and equally intense temper. The woman's smile had delighted Esther as a child and stirred feelings within that she had not understood until the day they first kissed under the shade of the orchard. Siobhan, who rode beside her, who loved her because of her passions and poetries and for both sides of her heritage, had converted from her father's faith so that there might be no god to stand between them.

Siobhan, at this very moment, was probably beating the stuffing out of some poor bastard who had no idea what he was in for, something Esther had requested their guards not bestir themselves over in past years.

Rolling her eyes, Esther walked to the building where she knew she'd find her companion. She passed a coin to the doorman before stepping into a smoke-filled den of cheers and shouts. Esther was soon standing upon a railing, overseeing a dirt pit below.

In the pit's southern corner was a slender, lean brute with wrapped knuckles and a scraggly beard. In the other, stripped to a vest and bindings upon her chest, red hair bound up like a coiled snake around her scalp, was Siobhan.

Esther sighed heavily and made her way through the yelling crowd. Some probably even remembered last year and were taking steps to bet accordingly. The pitmaster jotted down each wager with all the enthusiasm of a tired clerk working a long shift. Esther stepped up to him.

"Ten on the one with red hair," she remarked.

The man lifted an eyebrow but accepted the wager without much fuss. Interested in the outcome despite her brief exasperation, Esther strolled up to the railing and gazed down to enjoy the fight.

The lean man opened the match with several heavy blows, but Siobhan refused to put her fists down. She sidestepped, weaving in between his strikes. Esther's father had been a champion boxer while in the Union army and had trained both women accordingly. His chief lesson was that hunger drove any fight, whether the desire for land, money, vengeance or victory. In the mountains by Grey's Bluffs, their guards' people had fought many times to buy their territory in human blood before.

Esther briefly diverted her eyes from the fight to scan the room. The things from the Hungers were stealthy, though not enough to hide out in a crowded room.

Siobhan wanted it. She was dancing in between the blows, letting the man tire himself out by occasionally deflecting his strikes here and there. When his guard faltered, Siobhan saw her opening. She waltzed up and struck him in the face with the heel of her palm rather than her knuckles. She waltzed back from retribution, coming in for several jabs. Apparently, she felt like showing off, risky in a fight.

Esther pursed her lips in frustration while men and women shouted all around her.

Siobhan was a crowd favorite. Basking in the adulation, she drew the fight out, waiting until her opponent swung and overextended with the blow. She took a bold step closer, struck him in the chin and stepped back. It was just a tap, but he collapsed like a sack of flour.

The room stilled. Then everyone erupted with raucous cheers, the Irishwoman now a great favorite of the crowd.

"Hashem, gimme some strength, 'cause I need it sometimes," Esther mumbled under her breath.

***

"Ya liked it."

"I did not. That was just bein' careless and showin' off, Siobhan."

"Ya still liked it." Siobhan pushed Esther against the wall, a broad grin on her face. Dissatisfied with the money they already had, Siobhan had helped herself to a substantial payout from the pits. She was quite delighted with the amount her companion had won by betting on her. Siobhan leaned in and kissed Esther playfully, the two well-concealed from prying eyes.

"I think we got enough to buy Padraig and Lacey new saddles and oats. Not to mention a room for the night. We got time before ol' Abe's expectin' us back."

"If we ain't targeted by the folk who just lost money on ya." Esther wriggled free of her lover's grasp. "Ya ain't takin' things serious unless we're near the Hungers. Or did ya forget we're bein' watched this whole time? What if our friends forgot it was just a friendly match?" Esther lowered her voice. "I know ya told 'em not to get upset if someone smacked ya around in the ring a few years, but I don't fancy anyone comin' after us, nor riskin' anyone's life."

"First off, I think our protection's good for another little while, *metuka.*" Sweetheart was the nearest approximation in English. Siobhan loved her Hebrew endearments when she knew Esther was irritated. "'Til we get back home. Second, that fella was never gonna lay a hand on me. Third, they ain't gonna do a thing to any folks who ain't a real danger. Ya know how they are. Probably watchin' us right now."

"I'd rather not be reminded of that, thanks very much." Esther scanned the buildings, still seeing nothing. As good as the deals were, she did not like to think of the Hungers and the deals her father had made there. Few stories of the Hungers existed. Esther only knew what lay in those mountains predated humankind and any incursions never returned. She did not know if any of the tribes spoke of them. "Let's just get some food and rest, then head home. How about that?"

Esther centered her gaze back on Siobhan. The other woman's smile slowly faded, replaced by a touch of guilt passing over her face. Esther looked Siobhan straight in the eyes. "I ain't begrudgin' ya some fun here'n there. But trouble don't find us the same. I love ya dear, but ya have to remember that."

Chastened, Siobhan leaned in and pressed her forehead to Esther's. "I'm sorry, *metuka sheli.*" My sweetheart. It sounded so much lovelier in Hebrew.

Esther kissed Siobhan's cheek. "It's okay. Ya can't help showin' off. Just remember, I'm at more risk with folk than ya."

Siobhan did forget sometimes, having grown up in Grey's Bluffs. While her people had known hardship and discrimination, riots and violence, Siobhan had seen how much harder it was for those who shared Esther's heritage. "I'm sorry, Esther. Truly, I am. I was just tryin' to blow off steam."

"Ya did a fair job of it." Esther led Siobhan back out into the street. She could not stay irritated at her lover for long. "I say we get a room now."

The saloon door opened, and a man was hurled outward into the street. After him came a much larger man, his face twisted in fury as his foot slammed into the downed fellow's side again and again. The man on the ground doubled up, whimpering. The bigger man vented his fury on the prone figure, nobody interfering.

"Teach ya to take all that money," the bigger man said. "Musta cheated! I'll fix ya good!"

The smaller man was in danger of being seriously injured.

Esther suddenly recognized him. "Hey!" She took a step closer, trying to gauge the attacker. The man was bigger than her and Esther was not sure if he was armed. It was not the way she wanted to begin a confrontation. "That's enough!"

She recalled the assailant from the fighting pit. He had been in the other corner cheering on Siobhan's opponent when the fight started. When the fight ended, he'd been snarling in disappointment at the woman's victory.

The big man stopped his assault, looking at Esther with a baleful expression on his face.

Esther cleared her throat and made her way closer to the duo. "That you, Tobias?"

"M-Miss Esther?" Tobias clutched his ribs. It would be a miracle if they weren't broken. He attempted to scuttle close to Siobhan and Esther, wheezing for breath. "I didn't do nothin', Miss Esther. I swear it!"

"Easy now." Esther knelt and put a hand on the man's blond hair as if to forgive him of any wrongdoings. Tobias was an orphan who lived at Grey's Bluffs. The lad had a knack for getting into trouble at whatever town he wandered into. But he was loyal and Esther had no intention of letting further harm come to him. "There weren't no call for that, mister."

The man sneered at Esther, towering over her.

She let her hand creep toward her side where she had left her sidearm. The man shifted, exposing the gun at his own side. Esther realized this could turn very ugly very quickly. "Man did nothin' more than win a fair bet."

"Weren't nothin' fair about it, sure's my name's Mike Vinson," the man snarled. "That Irish witch cheated! We all saw it!" Vinson glared daggers at Siobhan. The man had all the fury of a drunkard missing his wallet before the final round.

Siobhan walked closer to Esther. Esther extended a hand, a silent plea for her lover to leash her own belligerence. Vinson had no idea how close his life was to forfeit now.

"Look, if it makes ya feel better?" Esther moved slowly so as not to arouse Vinson's suspicion. "How's about I give ya some of my own cash to settle things? Ya let Tobias here go, we all walk away nice and easy."

Vinson screwed his face up, peering at Esther. Her gold star dangled from her neck, Vinson's eyes centering on it. He brayed a laugh out. "Lookie there, one'a *them* offerin' money!" He roared it for the crowd, murmurs rippling through the people in attendance. Vinson jabbed a finger at Esther's face. "That ain't just some tan on ya, is it? Which was it, your pa or your mama?"

Esther saw Siobhan flexing her fists, hearing her lover control her breathing. Esther could tell Siobhan wanted nothing more in all the wide world than to introduce her fists to Vinson's face. After the man's proclamation, people were whispering to one another, some snickering with their eyes on Esther, who despised their stares. She tried to tell herself it didn't matter, even when she heard whispered speculation on her parentage in the crudest of terms. Others simply commented on her faith. If this escalated and she was forced to draw iron, there was little chance it could be deemed self-defense.

She swallowed her pride for all its bitter taste. "I'm just askin' ya to be reasonable. Tobias here is a fella from my town. He's just not good at stayin' outta trouble. Look, ya already kicked him around; he got it. I'm offerin' to give ya what's yours."

"I'll take it all then," Vinson growled.

Siobhan looked at her lover, seeking permission.

Esther shook her head, barely perceptible. "I'm doin' this for your sake." Esther knew how that had sounded, but Vinson took a step forward. He reached for her, and Esther balled a fist and readied to strike.

A hand closed on Vinson's shoulder from behind.

"Who the hell—?" Vinson turned, and a fist slammed into his face. The man went down hard, hitting the ground with a dull thump. He did not even try to get up again, laying on his face.

A man stood over him wiping his knuckles with a grunt of displeasure. He was tall, thin, with a lined and weather-beaten, clean-shaven face that had seen too many days of sunlight. His coat was black and red, identical to several men flanking him.

"Now, I know you weren't makin' trouble for these fine ladies here," the man said with a deep voice. "This here's the daughter of a hero, folks! A man who fought for his country! You all gotta treat that with some respect."

Esther studied the man, recognition sparking as he peered down at her. She looked into his eyes, recalling years before when her father had introduced her to men from the army. "We know each other, mister?"

"Hell, I ain't surprised you don't remember me. But there's no mistakin' that fire in you, nor the star 'round your neck. Somethin' you're all lookin' at?" The man shouted at the townspeople. "Damn well should charge ya admission at this rate! Get this piece of shit outta my sight and move on!"

Several men rushed to obey, the good Samaritan flashing white teeth in a smile, before glancing to Tobias. "He hurt there?"

"Ain't nothin'." Tobias wheezed as he clambered to his feet. "Just made a bet with the wrong fella. Esther and Siobhan bailed me out. Again," he added, sheepishly.

The stranger folded his muscled arms over a broad chest. "Esther indeed. Last time I saw you, you were yea high and fit to bounce on your daddy's knee! Name's Cyril, girl. Cyril Redstone. Boys with me are Percival Beard and Nicky Rackets."

"Cyril," Esther repeated the name, offering her hand.

Cyril took it with no hesitation, shaking her hand firmly right there in the street.

"I owe ya thanks," she said. "Coulda handled a drunken lout like that, but folk around might not see it our way. Appreciate ya steppin' in when ya did."

"Perish the damn thought, girl, I only did what any good American would do. Like I said, I owe your daddy my life." Cyril's grin grew broader. Esther could scarce imagine the chances of finding her father's old comrade here. Abraham would have said the Almighty moved in mysterious ways as explanation. "I see you're flush with cash, lass! And from what Percy tells me, he lost a bit bettin' against your friend there."

The stout Percival Beard was grumbling at that, evidently not as good a sport as Cyril. Rackets snickered, taking a swig from the flask at his hip.

Esther could not feel any malice from Redstone. "I thank ya again, Mr. Redstone."

"Just Cyril, girl. We're practically family. Your daddy talked about your mama like she was an angel sent from above. What're they up to lately?"

"My mama passed a long time ago. It's just us and the town," Esther said before she could stop herself. "I'm just performing a few errands is all."

"Well, I'm proper sad to hear that about your mama. May Christ rest her soul."

"All due respect, Cyril, she didn't believe that same way as most folk 'round here," Esther whispered. She had never known her mother's people, nor had she known her beliefs, but she felt the urge to defend her mother from that attempted intrusion, no matter how well meaning it was.

"Meant no disrespect," Cyril said quickly with a tip of his chin. His smile lingered, his eyes warm and friendly. "Ya headed back to your town after?"

"Soon enough," Esther remarked, casting an eye over Tobias and Siobhan. "Fella there is with us. Tobias, what brought you over here?"

"Just pickin' up supplies for the town, Miss Esther." Tobias winced gingerly from his bruises. The man who had assaulted him was being hauled to his feet by fellows wearing similar livery to Cyril's. "Sorry I can't even do that right."

"Don't let it trouble ya none, but no more gamblin'," Siobhan said, patting Tobias's shoulder.

The two women tended to look after the hapless lad. Esther's father had always taught her that it was the duty of those with authority, power, and the means to see after those they could. That was the promise of America, Abraham, claimed, even if the nation had so often failed to fulfill it.

"Well, Esther, if it please you, give your daddy my regards." Cyril's smile was the bright and innocent gleam of an old friend returned for an unexpected dinner. "It's been a long time, but also give my condolences regardin' your mama and my absolute respect on his flourishin' at town." Cyril's smile curdled slightly as he fixed the fallen belligerent with a dark look. "I'll have my boys look after Mr. Vinson there so he don't try nothin' stupid later. Anyone who lays a finger on you answers to me and mine. Ain't that right, Nicky?"

Nicky, wiped his mouth, placing his whiskey flask back at his hip after a long pull. "Oh, that's right, Cyril!" he said with a sniff. Nicky seized Vinson and hauled him over. "Enough trouble for one day, fella." He patted his back. "Don't be botherin' no ladies now."

Something about Cyril was too friendly. The kind mannerisms seemed a pantomime, like an actor reading from an unfamiliar script and doing his best onstage. The way he looked at Esther was not disquieting lust, nor haughty disdain. He did not seem entranced or repulsed by the star around her neck, nor the color of her skin. He simply watched her, studying her with a vague interest.

"I'll be passin' your regards to my father, Cyril." Esther held her hand out and Cyril took it once more. She squeezed firmly, demonstrating no weakness. "Ya take care now. Along with your boys."

"Mercenaries," Siobhan whispered as they walked off, leaving Cyril and the rest behind. She had a gentle arm around Tobias. "Those coats ain't for show, hon. Means there's likely more of 'em where we can't see 'em."

"I could tell," Esther whispered. She resisted the urge to glance back, inwardly relieved nothing had escalated to violence. She far preferred their guards from the Hungers have no cause to move on anyone. "What do ya think they're in town for?"

"Bustin' workers' skulls maybe." Siobhan's voice was thick with disdain. Esther remembered enough stories of Irish laborers and how their employers considered them expendable. "I'm not likin' the way that fella looked at ya."

"My father saved his life. I don't think he was lyin' about that much. But still, I say we slip outta town early, the three of us. Get to Grey's Bluffs and tell Daddy." Something occurred to Esther, and she scanned the rooftops for any sign of furtive movement. "We're only protected until we get back to town. That's the deal."

Abraham loved deals. Perhaps even more frightening than the Hungers was Gerard Bancroft and he'd worked out a bargain with him as well. He was very good at negotiations, her father. "Tobias, you can stay outta trouble for the night, can't ya?" She mussed his hair, laughing softly. The youth grinned at her from a bruised face. "Appreciate ya believin' in Siobhan, though. Let's get some rest and head back home tomorrow."

***

Blackhawks or no Blackhawks, Mike Vinson decided he would kill himself a few people that night.

While Todd the boxer had advised him to forget the women, taking his loss to the little Irishwoman far better than Mike had thought possible, a few mouthfuls of whiskey and time to stew on his public humiliation had given him the idea. It weren't right for no woman to speak to him that way, nor for the Blackhawks to swoop in and take their side. And it especially galled him they all did it to save that skinny little cheat of a boy.

Vinson paced the room he had purchased, the stench of whiskey permeating the air in a pungent aroma. He would kill them, Vinson rasped, telling himself the same thing over and over again. Vinson ambled along the length of the bed, looking at the revolver and the knife. He'd need to shoot the redhead first—in the stomach, so she'd bleed slow. The other one, the dark-skinned girl … he'd slit her throat; that was it. See how confident she talked with her lungs filling with blood. "I'm gonna kill 'em, then beat that little fuck to death with my bare damn hands," he said aloud.

"Will you now?"

Mike Vinson froze and turned to the window.

He was on the second floor of the hotel, but the voice had come from just outside, a breathy whisper forced through a mouthful of knives. Had the Blackhawks followed him? Were they watching him, protecting the girls for purposes he could not guess?

"Who's there?" Vinson could not keep a look of shock from his face, reaching for his revolver on sheer instinct. "Mr. Redstone? I was just funnin' there. Weren't nothin' meant by earlier!"

He tried to seize his gun but found he no longer had a hand with which to reach. Something lurched back, the window blowing the cold night air into his face. Vinson stared at the ragged tears of flesh that had once been a wrist, blood pumping from the wound, reminding him of the fresh springs of his youth. His heart, the battered well that it was, pumped frantically to replace the departing blood and Mike tried to scream.

One rustle of movement, one burst of agony, and he no longer had a tongue with which to do that. He toppled back, only then seeing the shape in the darkness of the room. The shape was broad, rising to a greater height than him. It lifted a hand and pinched between two sharp nails, through a decaying veil of sanity, Vinson saw his tongue.

It fed the tongue between rows of sharp teeth, the eyes burning like hot coals. It swallowed, a rumble of satisfaction rising from its throat. Looking into those eyes, Mike could only see the oldest and most primal of all emotions, what he had seen in men around a dinner table and coyotes ripping at hares in the desert.

It was on him before Vinson had time for any other thoughts. He couldn't scream anymore.

But he tried.

CHAPTER FOUR

Esther had sent for a hot bath early in the morning. Any potential questions about her sharing a room with another woman were deflected by claims Siobhan was her sister—coupled with extra payment. People learned not to ask questions when silence fattened their pockets.

Tobias was safely tucked away in a room down the hall, Esther and Siobhan relieved to not have to worry about him. Shortly after her request, the innkeepers had placed a thick and heavy wooden tub in the room, filling it with hot water. Esther had smiled, paid them extra from Siobhan's winnings and sent them on their way.

Now Esther was laying back in the tub, resting her head against Siobhan's shoulder as the waters soothed her tired muscles and washed away the dirt of the road. "This is nice."

"Just nice?" Siobhan's arms were around her, lips brushing against Esther's hair. Her skin was so warm against Esther's, one hand reaching down so she might link their fingers, pale skin to dark.

"It's wonderful. Which is nice." Esther put her head back against her lover's shoulder, exhaling deeply. She loved the feel of Siobhan's soft skin and the hard muscle beneath. She had completely forgotten the Blackhawks and Bancroft and even the notion of being followed and 'guarded.' "You're still a show-off."

"Don't act like ya don't like it." Siobhan tapped a finger on Esther's lips.

Esther caught the hand with the same swift pull she used when drawing a gun. She kissed Siobhan's bruised knuckles, exhaling softly. "Suppose we'd best get ready."

"I can't hold ya a bit longer?"

"Hold me all ya like and then some when we get back home. We don't wanna keep Tobias waitin'. Boy'd be in a heap of trouble without us."

"True." Siobhan reluctantly released her arms so Esther might pull herself from the tub.

Esther let herself drip dry before retrieving her clothing, an amused flattery crossing her face as Siobhan's admiring gaze followed her. "Don't wanna hear nothin' from ya right now, Siobhan."

"Sometimes there ain't a thing to say when you're lookin' at a work of art, darlin'." A trace of childhood brogue crept into Siobhan's voice and sent a shiver across Esther's spine.

"Flirt. C'mon, Lacey and Padraig are gonna be waitin' for us. Those horses have earned themselves sugar cubes and apples." Esther flicked her head. "Let's say shalom to this place 'til next time. Sooner we clear outta Bancroft's turf, the better. I'm sick of ridin' already."

Siobhan lifted herself from the tub, crossing to begin dressing as well. "I'm sorry again about yesterday, *ahuvati.*"

"Ya can say 'beloved.' I swear, all the Hebrew, no zeal like the convert." Esther pulled her lover in and slipped her arms around her, taking another long kiss that was harder to leave than even Siobhan's arms. "I forgive ya. Weren't no harm done. Ain't like ya wandered too close to the caves at the Hungers."

"Don't even joke about that one," Siobhan said as they collected their things. "Seen our friends?"

"No. I like it better that way." Esther knew their 'friends' could control their appetites, as they did every tributary period, but she hated that so many people in Independence might be at risk. "Sooner we're home, sooner they're gone."

They left their room and walked down the hall to knock on Tobias's door. The youth pulled himself out of his room, fully dressed, bright and eager with his eyes shining. "I'm ready! Got all my things back there, everything Mr. Foxman needs. I feel awful rotten about what happened yesterday, Miss Esther. I got too caught up."

"Lemme guess." Esther rolled her eyes. "Ya had a few drinks, thought ya might go 'round, ya saw Siobhan and thought ya could make a little profit bettin' on her. And then ya happened to say somethin' to the wrong fella, Mike Vinson back there."

Tobias's sheepish expression told her all she needed to know.

With a pat to his back, Esther flicked her head toward the stairs. "Ain't no harm done yet. We just get on the road and avoid any trouble 'til we're back at Grey's."

Esther would be especially happy when she was away from people staring at her. Not for the first time, Esther thought what her mother would have said to her now. She wondered if Halona had lived long enough, if Esther would have known her ways, and her mother's family. Esther had no idea if she still would be Jewish.

She refused to set aside her star, the heirloom passed down from parent to child for years. Jewish blood ran down from the mother, her father had told her. Halona had never been Jewish herself, but Abraham had still raised her in his ways. Perhaps that had been selfish of him. Had he been unable to find someone of his wife's people to educate Esther after their move west, or had it been unwillingness? Or had he been scared for Esther's safety? Jews were seen with suspicion by so many people back in the cities and the towns, but they were more tolerated than the men and women of the tribes.

Every time she went back into town, Esther had read of a new injustice. People who fancied themselves good Christian folk murmured approvingly to one another how the Natives were better off dead. Black men and women, Mexicans and Chinese folks, they were scarcely seen as human beings.

Esther tried to hold her head up with pride even so, proud of her faith and to be her mother's daughter. Things had to get better, she told herself. Esther hungered to live and see this country change.

She purchased provisions for the road, finding the three horses rested and ready. Three sugar cubes were provided as treats, Lacey bearing the extra weight of Esther and the money without complaint as a result.

Their protection from the Hungers lasted until they crossed the boundaries of Grey's Bluffs.

Without another word, they were out, leaving civilization, with all its flaws, behind them.

***

Cyril waited several hours until he was certain Esther and Siobhan were gone. He sat in a chair near the bed, wearing his coat and trousers. His eyes were on his revolver, resting unloaded on a small table. Bancroft had told him the boy Tobias was in town, along with his connection to Grey's Bluffs. From there, Cyril had just needed to send one of the

Blackhawks to offer him drinks until he gave information on his hometown without realizing it. Esther had been just a happy coincidence. Cyril truly was happy to see that lass again. She was tough, along with that pugilistic friend of hers. Cyril respected strength, wherever it might be found. If Cyril had it in him to regret anything, he would have regretted their forthcoming deaths. Killing them in town would have been problematic, but the Blackhawks had gotten enough information out of that Tobias boy that the little sot had not even realized he was giving.

Cyril had long since stopped contemplating why he did the things he did. Regret was a foreign thing to him, as distant from him as the notion of introspection. His profession was murder, his purpose the acquisition of wealth. He didn't think he would ever stop.

That was America. When you didn't have, you wanted. When you had, you wanted more.

"Cyril?" The knock at the door pulled him from his reverie. "Cyril, somethin' you might wanna hear."

"What is it, Ben?" Cyril asked, only mildly curious. "Other boys back from drinkin' and gettin' round?"

"Whole unit's ready, sir, all thirty of us! Though, uh, haven't been able to figure out who it was, but it kinda seems like someone took your orders on Vinson a little too serious."

Cyril halted, still as a week-old corpse. "Get in here and don't say another word until you do." The door swung open and a panicked looking Ben entered, shutting the door behind him. The man moistened his lips nervously, Cyril looking into his sun-darkened face without any expression. "Is this some attempt to pass the buck?"

"No, Cyril, ya know I'd never go behind your back or do anythin' ya didn't order."

"Lack of imagination is a quality I confess that I appreciate in my subordinates," Cyril remarked as he drummed his fingers upon his knee. "Out with it, Ben."

"Accordin' to the innkeeper down the street, Vinson's missin'."

"Did you really come to bother me because a useless drunk is off in a ditch somewhere?"

"The room was also drenched in blood. The innkeeper was proper torn about needin' new sheets."

"Probably more torn than anyone findin' themselves needin' a new Vinson." Cyril's eyes narrowed darkly and he rose to his feet, throwing off the coat to take up his shirt. This was a problem. Bancroft was bound to know by now about the confrontation in the street. The last thing Cyril needed was a public murder jeopardizing his relationship with a generous employer.

"So, when I said keep an eye on him and elaborated nothin' more?"

"Cyril, I spoke with Percy, with Nick, with Rich and Zeke, with Vic, with everyone! They took turns watchin' the door on that inn. There's only one way in and Vinson never came out. His room was on the other side on the second floor, no way could he have jumped out, there's no blood outside!"

"Sounds like a real mystery to me. What it don't sound like is my fault, and I plan to make sure Bancroft knows that." Cyril supposed someone in the inn could have killed Vinson. Hell, the damn innkeeper could've done it for all Cyril cared. Puzzling, but not exactly his first priority. "I'll tell the boys the whole plan when we get into this, Ben. If I find you're lyin' to me, though?"

Ben winced at that, finding the courage to look Cyril in the eye. "You'll kill me?" he asked meekly.

"I'll dock your damn pay," Cyril muttered, rolling his eyes. Shooting his own men could negatively impact employment rates in the Blackhawks. He liked his men mean and harsh, but that sadly did not always translate to intelligent conversation.

But that was all right. Cyril planned a very good talk with an old friend soon. "Ya probably don't want that, my friend." He smiled, dismissing Mike Vinson from his mind. "Cause when we get where we're goin'?" He lowered his voice. "Few folk told me the ladies were swappin' out gold for cash. There's a mine near that town. Up in them mountains. They come back every year. It's a reason they prosper, along with the trade lines. We get in there and we keep some alive … then we find them mines … We load ourselves up with more than we can carry and then we give the land to Bancroft & Hughes."

Ben looked uncomfortable, Cyril cocking his head. "What is it?"

"Me an' the rest … we're all in on this, Cyril, but this job at Grey's. That's over by the Hungers, Cyril."

"I am acquainted with the general geography in the area."

"They say an entire patrol went missin' 'round those mountains once! And then an entire host of outlaws. They say even the heathens won't go near it, that ya can hear howlin' there at night!"

Ben's eyes were wild, and Cyril cursed the superstitious nonsense of fools. "If there are coyotes and wolves up there, I guarantee you that hot lead'll stop 'em in their tracks."

He reached out and put a hand to Ben's shoulder. "There ain't nothin' we gotta worry about."

"But Cyril—"

"Shut the hell up when I'm talkin' to you. Plenty of folk must've had reason to kill Vinson. A pair of little girls had nothin' to do with it." Cyril's eyes narrowed darkly. "There's gold in them mountains, and I ain't lettin' ghost stories prevent you from doin' your job. You hear me?"

There was nothing that would stand between Cyril and his profit. Not the innocent lives of Grey's Bluffs. And especially not their ridiculous legends.

CHAPTER FIVE

Esther could not help but shiver in relief when they crossed the threshold into Grey's Bluffs. The stretch of fertile land filled her heart with joy, the buildings in the near distance making her long to return home quicker. Tobias rode close to them, waving to the farmers working the fields. Esther wheeled her horse off, sending Siobhan and Tobias ahead. She rode to the fields and the rocks, ready to finish the bargain.

She stopped near the rushes, reminding herself that their erstwhile guards were fully capable of blending close into the background when they so chose. "On behalf of my home and my family, I thank ya for your escort and your protection."

Sometimes they said nothing in response, leaving only a soft rustle of departure. This was not one of those times.

"As agreed. Until next time." The voice was a harsh whisper, summoned up from a throat that lacked for familiarity with the human tongue.

If she had any choice in the matter, Esther would have far preferred to travel unimpeded by the company of the Hungers' folk, unseen or no. She could only thank the Almighty she had never encountered any problems those things had deemed it necessary to 'deal with,' but just the knowledge they were close by could give a woman nightmares.

The Hungers were always visible in the distance, a grim reminder of what lay in those mountains. But they let Grey's Bluffs be. As long as no human being crossed the boundaries at the Hungers, everyone was content to leave it that way.

Esther caught Siobhan waiting for her on Padraig. She spurred Lacey on to greet the other woman, resisting the urge to kiss her in full view of the public. Everyone knew, but it was still something not discussed in polite society. Nevertheless, Esther rode with Siobhan's hand gripping her own, the two meeting Tobias in the boundaries of the settlement.

Years of work from Esther's father and many enterprising men and women alike had seen Grey's Bluffs raised into a thriving community within the shadows of the Hungers. Buildings sat all in rows, shops and homes neatly arranged one after the other. Farms lay on the outskirts of town, overseeing green fields. The foundations of new buildings had already been laid, animals grazing along the lands that were raised and bred for meat and milk. Esther passed the church and the synagogue, riding to the house on the edge of town. Here, nobody glanced at her with suspicion or distaste. Here, she received shouts of her name and joyous waves, Siobhan laughing happily.

"Shalom!" Siobhan called to Esther as they reached the Foxman home.

The building lay on the west side of town, erected by Abraham himself. Two stories tall and dark wood with their land and animals out in back. Esther bid Tobias farewell to his own home before she and Siobhan left Padraig and Lacey in their stables with enough oats for food to accompany their rest.

"Esther!" The deep voice called.

Esther turned to see the man exiting the house, a smile on his weathered features. Her father's black hair was going gray, years on the frontier leaving his face worn and tan. His hazel eyes still sparkled with youthful enthusiasm, his body lean and strong from the labor he refused to give up despite his wealth.

"Come here!" He opened his arms, and Esther raced into them, just as she had when she was a little girl. Abraham laughed and enfolded his daughter within his embrace, his stubble tickling her cheek.

Esther batted him off, teasingly tapping her hands to his shoulders. "It's good to see ya, Daddy," she said brightly, smiling fondly at him.

"Wonderful to see you home, my love." Abraham still spoke like he was from Pennsylvania while Esther and Siobhan had adopted the thicker tones of the western country. He put a hand to her cheek. "There were no problems?"

Esther thought about telling him of Mike Vinson and the bruises he'd left on Tobias. "Nothin' we couldn't handle. Some fool got a little rough with Tobias. Fella didn't lay a hand on us."

"Fortunate for him he did not," Abraham murmured, casting his eyes behind them in the direction of the Hungers. *"Todah rabah."* A quick prayer of thanks, more intended for the Lord above than for Esther herself. "I hope Tobias is not badly hurt."

"Few bruises, silly lad'll live." Esther cast a glance to Siobhan hurrying over. "Nothin' much else I can report to ya. We got our money; it's here for when your traders show up and Mr. Bancroft'll be happy. We did run into an old buddy of yours, though."

Abraham paused briefly to envelop Siobhan in the same warm hug he had given Esther. He whispered an endearment in Hebrew, Siobhan repeating it back before they released one another.

"Said his name was Redstone," Siobhan said. "Cyril Redstone."

"Cyril indeed?" Abraham lifted an eyebrow. "I haven't heard that name in a long, long time now."

"Seemed a little over-familiar, if you ask me. Was wearing mercenary clothin', Daddy," Esther said, recalling the trail-beaten face of her father's old friend. "He mentioned he was in the army with ya? That ya saved his life?"

"At Antietam … That is correct," Abraham agreed. He touched his chin, rubbing it slowly, as though steadily chewing upon the thought like a particularly savory hunk of meat.

"I can't say I've heard much of Cyril. Nor did he ever give me cause for concern when we served together. I hosted him a few nights years ago when you were a little girl, Esther, but nothing more than that. I'm glad you made it back without incident. The town is expanding and thriving as well, I'm happy to say. Shabbat isn't far off and we can look forward to a great and bountiful Passover." He put a hand to Siobhan's head and affectionally toyed with her hair. "I'm thrilled to report I have a fair supper prepared tonight. I'm truly grateful for your efforts at the Hungers, Esther. It pleases me our friends weren't much a bother. The traders will be by in just a few days and we can purchase enough goods to last the town a good, long while."

"Be glad for dinner, that's for sure." Esther was proper starved when she thought of it. So eager had she been to depart Independence, she had barely managed a meal. "I'll fill up some water from the back after, if you need me to help."

"Don't be silly. I'm not so old I can't handle this." Abraham slipped an arm around his daughter's shoulders. "You've been working nonstop, and ranching will be there tomorrow and the next day. I'll trust you to deliver some new heads of cattle to their destination. Only after you've had a chance to rest, of course. Allow me to ensure you have no concerns tonight."

It was indeed a blessing to be back in a familiar house, Esther decided when she marched up the stairs to her room. Technically, Siobhan's was right across the hall, but it was rarely slept in. Esther's bed was big enough for two, a small grace offered by her father without ever needing a single word exchanged between them. Esther was grateful to remove her trail-dusted clothing, a fresh basin of water having been left for her. She began to wash herself, already thinking of the chance for a new bath before she dried herself and dressed in a new shirt and pants.

She removed her gun but kept it unloaded and in a safe place, pleased she had not had to use it on anyone or anything this time. The knock at the door snapped her from a brief reverie. "I'm decent here! Siobhan, ya come on in." She turned, seeing her father framed in the doorway instead. "Oh, Daddy. Everythin' all right?"

"I wanted to ask you that," Abraham said gently, his lips pursed. "I saw Siobhan's knuckles were bruised. Was there any trouble? Be honest with me this time, Esther."

"Like I said, it was nothin' we couldn't take care of," Esther said.

Abraham was studying her, as though deciding if he actually believed her.

"She just had a little fight for fun. That was all. A fella got a little rowdy after but your old friend prevented things from getting' outta hand."

Abraham sighed heavily. "I see," he remarked, looking into his daughter's eyes.

Esther tilted her chin back, trying to parse his feelings through his gaze. "I ain't a little girl no more. Just say what's on your mind."

"I worry sometimes I put too much on you. I know the pact demands me or mine adhere, but sending you to Independence, I confess, weighs upon me. It's why I sent Tobias to at least handle some of the errands."

Esther found it within herself to ask the questions she wanted. "Is that 'cause I'm a woman? Is it 'cause I like women? Is it 'cause of this?" She took hold of the star around her neck, before squaring her jaw. "Or is it 'cause of how I look? Ya think I don't hear what some folk say behind my back?"

"In Independence, or here?" Abraham kept his voice measured, no emotion showing on his face. "I tried to make Grey's Bluffs a sanctuary for our people, a place we might be free. There is no place for that talk here."

"Place or no, it's still here." Esther walked to her bed and sat there, brushing her hair back from her face and massaging her forehead. "What, do you wanna hide me away from the world? Act like I can't ever be in danger?"

"Of course not. I am not ashamed of you. Your mother wasn't either. Halona only ever wanted the best for you." Abraham walked closer to her, a deep sigh emanating from his lungs. "It's not you at fault. If the country denies you, then they're the ones who are wrong. Our people have been persecuted, driven from our homes, for thousands of years. There is no cause for any of us to look down on others. None. If you hear such whispers, I will put a stop to them immediately."

Esther knew her father wasn't ashamed. That was not the source of the sudden discontent she felt. "We're Jewish, Daddy. So's Siobhan. We don't fit with most white folk. But she fits in better with them than I can." Esther turned her eyes upward to the wooden ceiling. "Ya can make them stop talkin', but not thinkin'. Just livin' has its own dangers. And Mama …" Esther hesitated just a moment. "I don't remember her. Not the way I'd like. I never learned about the Creek or their ways, and …" She looked at her father closely. "Would ya have preferred I was Jewish before I was Creek?"

Abraham took another deep breath. There was no anger or offense in his eyes or on his face. "Your mother and I never wanted anything but for you to choose. Do you resent it?"

"No." Esther said it firm and clear. She took hold of her star again, holding it tight. "I'm proud of it. I'm proud to be Creek, too. No matter how they look at me or what anyone says, I'm glad for all I am. I just wonder what might've been different. Just sometimes."

"I'm sorry I don't have the answers." Abraham put an arm around Esther and hugged his daughter. "I didn't feel it was my place … passing on what should have been hers."

"Ain't nobody much left to pass it on that I've seen." Esther did not entirely succeed at keeping the bitterness out of her tone. She knew her father heard it, but Abraham gave no sign of offense. He squeezed her shoulder gently.

"I asked Siobhan to wait downstairs. Would you still care to join me for dinner?"

Abraham was dodging the issues because he had no easy answers. She managed to smile even so, leaning into him for another hug. He gave the only hugs he ever did, big and warm. "Life was easier when you thought I was omniscient."

"Watchin' ya make all the deals ya did sure helped with that." Esther patted his arm. "How did ya manage to pull it off with our friends in the mountains, anyways?"

"The people, if you wish to use that word, of the Hungers are reasonable. And usually hungry," Abraham said with a conspiratorial smile. "You might even say one of their number owed me a debt when we made our deal. They're territorial and not very friendly, but … they're reasonable. They didn't give you any problems?"

"They didn't eat anyone if that's what ya mean. No offense, but I kinda hate I have to worry about that."

"As long as nobody tried to hurt you," Abraham began, prompting a groan from Esther.

"Then nobody had reason to worry, I know! I heard it all before. Don't mean I gotta like 'em."

They sat in silence for several moments, Abraham's hand rubbing against her back. "Are you well now, Esther?"

She considered it for a moment. "Guess all I can do is go on livin' best I can." Her stomach growled a moment later, prompting a soft chuckle from her father. "Guess we shouldn't keep dinner waitin' then."

***

Cyril Redstone saw the towering majesty of the Hungers in the distance. In their shadow was Grey's Bluffs, the Blackhawks overlooking the town from the hills. No walls, scant defenses, but according to the foolish boy Tobias, there were a fair few who were former soldiers and the ladies alone were skilled hands with weaponry. The Blackhawks were trained killers to a man, but they were outnumbered by a fair amount. They'd have to hit hard and hit fast.

His eyes narrowed on the town. Nicky Rackets and Percy Beard waited at his side. Nicky was sober, a rare enough occurrence. Cyril needed every man focused on the job at hand. The Blackhawks looked hungry for plunder and murder alike.

Cyril drew his revolver to accentuate his point. "We ride down. I want ten to hit the front, six to the east, six to the west. The rest ride through town and start scarin' people. Flush 'em all out into the open, same as always." Cyril looked down the line, saw how the Blackhawks were passing torches to be bound with cloth and to be set alight. They already knew to hold off until they were in full gallop so that they were not seen and identified too early. "Burn as much as ya can. Burn 'em in their homes, in their beds. Kill everythin' that walks or crawls but leave enough left alive to talk. Make sure there are people to use as leverage to loosen some tongues too." People had a habit of being freer with information when they worried about their loved ones.

Percy grinned, flashing pearly teeth through his ridiculous little goatee. He drew his own gun, the chrome flashing silver by torchlight. "We all gotcha, Cyril! We goin' now?"

"That's right. You all know what to do." Cyril drove his feet into his mount's side with a whistle. The horse broke into an even pace, Cyril leading the Blackhawks from the hills to the flat plains. He could already see the farm fresh lands, Grey's Bluffs having prospered well, indeed. He thought of Abraham Foxman and how so much time had passed. The man had done better for himself than Cyril had.

He wondered how much blood Abraham had shed to satisfy his own hungers deep within. The smile stretched on his face as he prepared himself. There was no hatred for his victims, no malice in his heart. Cyril Redstone was beyond those as surely as he was beyond mercy.

Chapter Six

Esther was finishing a meal of hearty stew, washing it down with fresh well water, when she heard the gunfire.

Abraham froze in his seat for only a moment, leaping to his feet. "Were you followed?"

Esther's mind immediately went back to the man in red and black. "No." She shook her head frantically, disbelief settling as she desperately tried to replay the events of the past several days in her mind over and over. She thought of their time at the Hungers, their ride into Independence, and everything that had followed.

And Cyril Redstone.

Just the thought of him twisted her stomach. The realization of who was behind the gunfire struck her and she could see from her father's eyes, he had the same thought. Siobhan sprang to her feet, horror visible on her face.

Abraham crossed from the table to the wall and seized the rifle he kept there. "I need you both to arm yourselves." The thunder of gunfire arose again, coupled with screams. "Assess the circumstance as fast as you can and rally the others. Do you know how many there are?"

She shook her head frantically.

Her father displayed no panic, methodically beginning to load his rifle. "Esther, Siobhan, do as I say with no delays."

Esther ran upstairs to their room and collected her revolver from where she had left it. She took up her bullets, opened the chamber and loaded it quickly. More gunshots sounded, the screams outside suddenly silenced.

She heard hooves pounding the soil, loud shouts of triumph. Surely this would not stand, she told herself. Grey's Bluffs was protected, her bodyguards would deal with this.

But then Esther remembered the exact words of the pact.

Their protection was only good until they returned home. The people of the Hungers had departed, would not be coming to save them. She almost dropped her revolver, her legs weakening as tears flooded her vision. A sudden terror overtook her, and she was dimly aware of hands seizing her shoulder, Siobhan's voice calling her name.

She turned to face Siobhan, frozen in abject horror, expecting a slap so she might recover her wits. Instead, Siobhan kissed her forehead. "I know. I know. I'm scared, too. Focus with me, Esther. I can't do this without ya. Okay?"

Looking into Siobhan's eyes, Esther managed to take up the courage Siobhan had found for them both. Her father was out there. Esther's town was out there, its people at risk. "Okay," she said, her voice a hollow croak.

"Good." Siobhan pressed her forehead to Esther's before separating, tearing down the stairs with Esther at her heels.

Esther's heart pulsed up into her throat and she felt vomit rise. She could only replay the meeting with Cyril in her head, wondering how this had come to pass.

Cyril Redstone was a mercenary. Who could—

Bancroft. The answer came to her like a thunderbolt exploding into her brain. The man had not been satisfied with a cut after all. He wanted the entire pie.

All through Grey's Bluffs, the men were arming themselves, emerging from homes with their guns. But they were fighting in the dark, and the blazing flames from the burning buildings were hindering their vision. She saw familiar men and women running panicked in the streets, some falling as bullets ripped through them. Some were armed, holding themselves upright and finding cover to try to reach their opponents and take aim.

The mercenaries were everywhere, riding through town with cold professionalism as they shot down every last civilian of Grey's Bluffs whether they fought back or not. Somehow, they knew the layout of the town. There was no aid forthcoming, nobody close enough to the settlement to help. The folk of the Hungers were not coming. Maybe they didn't even care.

Esther heard her father shout, rallying the townsfolk. She joined them with Siobhan, but she could scarcely see a thing in the night. The revolver trembled in her hands, the crackle of the flames drowning out her father's voice.

Abraham was a soldier yet. He lifted his rifle, taking aim, and pulled the trigger. A scream and a thump rang out, a man toppling from his saddle. "Put your backs to something, find cover!" Abraham roared. "Esther, we'll take their fire, try to guard the civilians!"

It was pure chaos. There was no way Esther could have corralled everyone. It was equally impossible for anyone to escape. She heard Lacey screaming in her stables, animals panicking at the sounds of gunfire. It occurred to her with a sickening realization that even if Grey's Bluffs prevailed, many of their people would die. Their peace was at an end, their very way of life torn apart for the greed of Gerard Bancroft and Cyril Redstone— another dark page in the history of their people.

Esther's ears rang as the citizens opened fire, Abraham directing them like a general. Some fired in an attempt to give time for others to reload, knowing they wouldn't hit anything. The mercenaries returned fire soon after, the resistance pulling themselves around the buildings.

Shrieks echoed in the night, civilians and fighters alike having been run down. Esther heard pounding feet, followed by hooves. A group of people ran past her, pursued by men on horseback.

Her body was moving before her mind could keep up. Esther raced around the corner of one building, ignoring her father's shout to stay down. She lifted her revolver, planted her feet and recalled her training by the stables blasting empty bottles. The fires nearby illuminated her target, and she pulled the trigger.

The man's head exploded. He fell from his saddle, a forgotten sack of bone and viscera.

Esther paid him no further mind.

She raised her voice, shouting to be heard over the screams, trying to restore some semblance of order in the midst of chaos. The people looked to her, terror illuminated on their faces by the dancing flames. Esther heard someone shout her name, a man pushing through the crowd to stumble at her feet. She recognized Tobias instantly, his face streaked with tears.

"Miss Esther," he gasped, a man near him weeping with fear. "They're all dead, everyone. They just came outta nowhere ... I'm sorry!"

She pointed her hand back in the direction she had come. "My father's over that way. They're fightin' best they can! It'll be safest if ya hide somewhere, the lot of ya!"

"They're burnin' the town!" One woman protested. "Ain't nowhere safe!"

"Then find somethin' they haven't burned and hope we kill 'em all before they do!" As far as plans went, it wasn't the best, but Esther could think of nothing else.

Siobhan emerged from around the corner, rifle upon her shoulder to brace. She fired the repeater once, twice, two shouts informing Esther that she'd hit her targets. "Come on," Esther's lover yelled, her hair loose and tangled. She met Esther's eyes, panting raggedly. "Your daddy thinks you're a damn fool for runnin' out there and he's proud of ya."

Esther opened her mouth to respond when an explosion of gunfire sounded in the direction where they had left Abraham and the rest. The flames burned brighter, but the Blackhawks were pressing the assault with greater intensity than before. It was as if they were aiming to finish the fight now.

Through the fires, she saw him, striding forth, not on horseback, but on his bare feet. Cyril Redstone walked through the flames as though flanked by Hell's own legions. His gun was in his right hand and each bullet he fired was the conclusion to a man's life. His men were with him, firing wildly, and Esther could tell Grey's Bluffs was running out of defenders.

She had no clear shot at Cyril, not with gunfire ringing and her ears burning. She tried to take aim at his head, only for another man to step in the way. Her bullet didn't even kill him. It only winged his arm and made him yelp.

Cyril turned just as Siobhan lifted her own rifle, firing off a quick shot. The barrel of Siobhan's rifle exploded, leaving her with nothing but a useless stick of wood and metal. Men were firing, forcing Esther and the rest to retreat. Esther could not see her father, had no idea if he was alive or dead as bodies piled up in the streets. She could only hear the men closing in on her and the others, laughing in triumph.

***

Cyril Redstone saw a twitch from the corner of his eye and with a soldier's instincts, he threw himself to the side. That was all that saved his life when Abraham Foxman took the shot. The bullet blasted harmlessly through the door of a burning building. Cyril prepared to return fire, but Foxman hurled his rifle at Cyril's face, forcing him to slap it away.

There was only one reason for a damn fool move like that; the man was out of bullets. Unfortunately for Cyril, the desperate attack managed to ruin his balance for just a vital moment. That was all Foxman needed. Foxman charged immediately, crashing into Cyril. He slammed his old comrade into the dirt, the wind leaving Cyril's lungs. Stunned and lying on the earth, Cyril could only wonder where his men were when he needed them.

Foxman's face twisted in pure fury as he put his hands against Cyril's throat. This was not in the script.

Cyril gurgled, legs kicking as he thrashed, looking into Foxman's eyes. His hands beat the earth, an idea coming to Cyril just then. He seized a handful of sand and threw it in Foxman's eyes.

The man reared back and Cyril was up, sucking in ragged breaths of air. He flung a punch into Foxman's face, driving him back. His revolver had fallen free after Foxman's charge and Cyril lunged for it. He came up, aiming as he did, intending to kneecap his opponent. Foxman was too quick for him.

It had been twenty years since the war, but Foxman was still a boxer with a soldier's instincts. He hit Cyril's hand, knocking the gun to the dirt, launching a flurry of savage blows across his opponent's body that Cyril could only barely block.

Driven back from Foxman's assault, he tried to go for his knife, but Foxman was giving him no reprieve. It had been too long since Cyril had faced a man who could fight back. Ranching life had not softened his old comrade.

"Nice t'see you, too, Abe," Cyril managed, countering one blow and darting under a haymaker, only to catch a blow to the jaw that made stars explode in his vision. Cyril lunged back, shaking off the swimming in his skull.

The fight ended in moments. Cyril tried to fight back, but Foxman's blows made his ribs shake and his breath wheeze. The punches to the face that followed took all the remaining fight out of Cyril, and he fell to the ground, trying to scramble away.

Foxman didn't say a word. He strode forth to finish the job, but Cyril had reached what he needed. He rolled over, revolver at the ready, firing wildly. The shot caught Foxman between the neck and shoulder, making him fall back with a pained grunt.

Cyril heard the cries of men rushing up, Percy yelling his name. "Cyril, Cyril … Are you okay?!"

"No thanks to any of you!" Cyril swayed on his feet with none of his usual poise. Foxman lay on the ground, a hand to the injury with dark blood seeping out from between his fingers. "Now. As I was sayin' before. It's damn nice to see you, Abe."

"Cyril," Foxman whispered. His teeth bared in the gleam of the firelight. "I see gratitude has gone out of style."

"Now, Abe, that ain't fair. I'm proper grateful for what you did for me back at Antietam and all the times after.

Which is why I'm gonna give you a fair chance to save yourself some pain. The gold, Abraham … Where is it?"

"I have no idea what you're talking about."

Abraham was stubborn; Cyril could give him that. The victorious mercenary drew his knife slowly, letting the metal hiss from its sheath like an uncoiling serpent. "We saw 'em at Independence, Abraham. The lil' lad Tobias weren't too smart with reining in his tongue. Your little girl didn't screw up none, though, if it helps. Sorry about your lady, by the by."

He knelt over Foxman, his knife teasing the man's cheek. "I'm gonna get my answers, Abe. If it ain't you, I'll make your girl lead me to 'em."

"The mountains," Foxman whispered, a chuckle brewing in his throat. A look of defiance hung on his face, wholly unsuited to the situation at hand "You can go to the mountains. You'll find it there."

"Where in the mountains, Abe? I respect a good fight. I don't want to start cuttin' you, but I will if you make me."

"Make you?" Foxman refused to stop with that accursed glare. "Men like you always blame others, Cyril. You'll find everything you're looking for in the mountains. That's all I have for you."

Cyril wasn't certain that Abraham Foxman regretted much about his life. But he would make damned sure Foxman regretted Cyril's bullet had not killed him instantly before the end.

CHAPTER SEVEN

"What're they gonna do to us?" Tobias whispered.

Esther stood by him with Siobhan and the rest. They had been relieved of their weapons, which were now piled up in the middle of the town square with the corpses still around. The Blackhawks had formed a ring about the survivors, daring them to put a toe out of line. Esther had not seen her father, and she tried to remember the last words they had said to one another, but could not. Siobhan was with her, though, arms on her shoulders as Esther wept with helpless frustration. She wanted to be brave. Her mother would have been.

The Blackhawks watched with cold smirks, Esther resisting the urge to hurl insults at them. She bit back her temper, knowing that others might pay the price for her defiance. Esther had to think of Siobhan, of all who were still alive. Tobias was weeping, something in the lad's face beyond terror.

"We gotta thank ya," one of the men said, withdrawing a flask from his waist to take a gulp. "Lad of yours there sure talks a lot when he gets to the drinks."

Esther turned to Tobias, face expressionless. "What's he talkin' about?"

Tobias could not look at her, a pained grimace spreading over his face. "I … I'm sorry, Miss Esther. I am, honest. They just bought me a drink or two, asked where I was from. I didn't think … I didn't think anythin' bad would come of it!"

Siobhan seized him by the coat, yanking him close. Her face was a mask of molten fury. "What did ya tell them?" Her voice rose in a fevered pitch. "Tell me or by god, you won't need them to kill ya!"

The Blackhawks laughed uproariously at that. The man with the flask slapped it against his knee as if it was the funniest thing he had ever seen.

Tobias shrank away from Siobhan's wrath. All the survivors were now staring at him with equal rage. "I just told them a bit about the town, that's all," the lad moaned. "I didn't mean … I'm sorry, Miss Siobhan …"

Siobhan drew back her fist, but Esther seized it. "Let him go, Siobhan." Her voice was soft.

"Esther, he—"

"They would've done this no matter what he said or did. He was just stupid, not evil. Siobhan?" Esther fixed her lover with a commanding gaze, delivering an order in the most authoritative tone she could manage. "Let him go. Now."

Siobhan let Tobias fall to the ground, Esther sweeping her eyes to the others.

"Nobody's touchin' him, ya got me? We're stickin' together through this. It's all we got."She saw the ring of Blackhawks parting to allow several others through. There he was, his coat flapping in the breeze as the sun began to crest overhead. Esther stood upright, facing Cyril Redstone with all the courage she could muster. The only witnesses to her defiance of the Blackhawks were the few dozen remaining men, women, and children of Grey's Bluffs. Cyril threw something to the ground.

Esther looked down upon the sand. The blood-stained star she saw was a mirror of the one she wore around her neck. She did not scream, beg, nor rage. It was nothing more than the period at the end of a sentence, a confirmation of what she already knew.

"He died real quiet like, if it's any consolation to you," Cyril Redstone said. "Only gave up the ghost not long ago. Took us a while to finish off the wounded, but nobody else was talkin'. I suppose that makes ya the one in charge now, Esther."

Esther took a step forward, to the hoots of the Blackhawks. Cyril lifted an eyebrow. "Well, I'll be! Little half-breed Jew girl has got more stones than half my boys." He chuckled unpleasantly. "I hope you don't blame the lad back there. I'd rather that not bother you in this time of mournin'. You got several of my boys, Esther, more than I expected. But there's more than enough left to kill anyone here who even thinks of resistin'."

Siobhan seethed at her side, but Esther tilted her chin to stare Cyril Redstone in the eyes. "What are ya?"

"Hungry," Cyril returned. "And I hear the Hungers are what can fix that. I told your daddy he could get off light if he told us where it was. Money's nice, but gold's got a ring to it, girl."

"Ya damn fool, there ain't nothin' there for ya!"

"That's a matter of opinion, Esther, and I'm afraid we're gonna have to agree to disagree," Cyril remarked.

Esther remembered what her father had told her: the Hungers were no safe place for any man to tread, even fulfilling the pact could be perilous. The 'folk' there took retribution in full, and if they felt slighted. There was no guarantee they would cease their retribution with just the offending party.

"I'm gonna give the lot of ya a chance before I start cuttin' to see who knows somethin'. What's hidden here, in what houses, in what mines? I just killed a whole town, little girl. I just carved a man I owed my life to like he was a Sunday roast. Don't think there's a place I won't go to."

Esther knew he wasn't bluffing. She could see it in his pitiless eyes, more cougar than anything human. She silently bid Siobhan to stay where she was, not wishing for her lover to expose any vulnerabilities. "You'll kill us all, anyways."

"Dyin' has a certain spectrum to it, Esther. And it ain't like I gotta kill the lot of ya. Come on, what's a few Hebrews to anyone else?" He looked at them all, clicking his tongue softly. "The lot of ya disappear and maybe we can let bygones be bygones when I report back to Bancroft. What's it all to ya, Esther?"

She straightened in response, her teeth clenched as she found the courage, plucked it from her pumping heart. "My name is Esther Foxman. My father was Abraham Foxman. My mother was Halona of the Muscogee Creek. My father's people stood with Judas Maccabeus, my mother's with Tecumseh. Through generations, they fought to the last breath against men like ya, Cyril. And I ain't givin' you a damn inch."

Cyril nodded, looking genuinely impressed for a moment. "Real pretty speech." Then his fist struck her in the side of the head.

***

Perhaps the most perfect of metaphors for America that Cyril Redstone could have ever imagined was the splash of blood now staining the pale clay of the cold earth before his feet. Grey's Bluffs had been such a pleasant little settlement out in the deep frontier before Cyril and his men arrived, leaving ruin and devastation with only the stars and waning gibbous moon as witnesses to what the Blackhawks had wrought. Cyril's heart was nothing but hard leather, but were he capable of pity, he might have found some of it for brave little Esther Foxman. She now lay on the ground before him, learning for all her bold and pretty words, reality had a different perspective in mind.

A job was a job, and Bancroft & Hughes was paying top dollar to handle the recalcitrant townsfolk. Cyril was not letting speeches by some little playacting girl ruin his chance for a payout. Dirty business was what America was all about. It was a lesson as old as this nation, built upon lead and gun smoke: hunger drove everything. Cyril had learned that in the military before he decided he and his boys could get better pay as soldiers of fortune. There were always men with full pocketbooks and empty souls in need of such services. Cyril had achieved everything he had set out to, minus the little nature of secrets Abraham Foxman had taken to the grave.

Abraham had been a proud bastard, and stubborn as a damned ox. Cyril had spent a long time carving at the man, but he had refused to yield anything but cryptic remarks about the mountains before finally expiring.

Usually torture didn't work very well, not physically. But Foxman had barely been fazed by it, even when Cyril threatened to harm the others. And Cyril, having taken a beating himself, had been a bit *ornerier* than he might have otherwise.

The boys took their time going from house to house, while a few kept an eye on the survivors being held in the town square. Esther was a spitfire, indeed. He had to nip her defiance in the bud or some of her people might have found it in themselves to get stupid and heroic.

The young woman lay on the ground, one hand clasping tight to a six-pointed star around her neck. Her eyes fixed on Cyril with hate and determination, a heat so intense that he almost wondered if the distant mountain snows might melt.

"Esther," Cyril called, the smile of a job half-done lighting his grizzled features. "I'm sorry 'bout that punch there, but you're actin' like your daddy. He never did know when he should comply. I know I said you'd grown last time, but I didn't see how much until now. Come on, Esther, it's over, even Abraham would've seen that. Haven't you heard the times are changin', Esther? There's no room for wild antics anymore."

The other woman, Siobhan, was on her knees beside Esther, hand to her cheek. Her own face was pinched with sorrow and rage that mirrored Esther's. She wrapped her arms around the heiress of Grey's Bluffs, whispering tender words into her ear. Her hand came to Esther's hair, stroking delicately.

Now this intrigued Cyril. He had judged them to be simple comrades in arms prior to this moment, good friends perhaps, but this … Cyril was a well-traveled man of no minor education. He did not much care who loved who, what color a human was, nor what they said in prayers. He'd killed everything that walked or crawled for country and private industry, but it all amounted to earning a few extra clinks to his coins. Cyril was a modern man for a modern time. All he cared about was that these ladies had just exposed their weakness.

He lifted his gun, bringing it in line with Siobhan's knee. "Esther," he said in a tone as delicate as a crushed wildflower. "You show more sense than your daddy did, I might see fit to let you live, long as you clear out. Ya decide to be as stubborn as he was, I'll kneecap her right in front of you. Then I'll start cuttin' 'til that fair skin of hers runs red as her hair."

"Don't ya touch Siobhan," Esther snarled, pulling her closer, boldly shifting to place herself in front of the redhead. Her cobalt eyes blazed defiance.

Cyril respected that. These ladies were strong women, their bodies lean and muscled from hard work. Doubtless, they could ride well, judging by the many horses and cattle herd nearby.

"Swear to the Almighty, Cyril Redstone, ya put a finger near her, I'll bite your damned throat out!"

Cyril was pleased his instincts had proven correct. "Esther, I'm offerin' a bit of generosity on account of your most recent loss. I figure you got 'til the count of ten."

The Blackhawks let loose with a chorus of low chuckles. The survivors were being stripped of anything deemed valuable, Cyril had ordered them to delay any final massacre for the moment. As he had learned from trial and error, folks were more loose-lipped when someone they cared about had their head on the chopping block.

This was a flourishing settlement and the Foxman ranch was far wealthier than it had any right to be. That meant there had to be more nearby, more than the meager dollars Nicky Rackets and Victor Munson had just ransacked from their homes. There were some jewels as well, but one look at that mountain and Cyril just knew the people here had taken from those mines. Cyril was slightly irritated with himself for being so eager to put his knife into Foxman. He should have used Esther's life to threaten the man.

Cyril Redstone was not a man given to repeating his errors, even when his hunger for riches got the better of him.

"Time's up, Esther." He pointed the gun at Siobhan's kneecap.

The woman braced herself for the shot. Esther seized her shoulder as if her grip could transfer strength into her lover. Cyril wrapped his finger around the revolver's trigger. He began to squeeze.

"Wait!" The call came from Tobias's throat, the stupid boy so easily duped by the Blackhawks. The boy stared up at Cyril with desperation in his wild eyes.

Cyril slid his finger away from the trigger, though he kept the gun leveled at Siobhan's knee.

"Don't hurt Siobhan or Esther," Tobias said. "I'm beggin' ya! I promise, I'll give ya everythin' ya want."

Well, well, if it wasn't their little patsy. Cyril was proper tickled to see the boy still breathing and in good spirits. What's more, he was offering to lead them to what they wanted. The stupid little sot was proving very useful.

"Tobias, don't ya give them a damned thing!" Esther pulled herself to her feet with Siobhan, the two women still holding one another with the flames of defiance not yet quenched.

Cyril let himself smile, an ugly cupid bow of delight at the drama in which he found himself observing.

"Don't tell 'em about the mountain! They can search for the rest of their days for all I care!" Esther released Siobhan, taking a step forward.

"That's enough outta you!" Percy was always one of the Blackhawks packed full of more arrogance than good sense. He sauntered forth and lifted a hand to Esther without waiting for Cyril's permission.

Siobhan lunged at Percy and punched with the married grace of dancer and boxer. Beard's nose broke with the crunch of a shattering shot glass. He fell back, making sounds more fit for pigs than humans. The men roared with laughter and approval for Percy's misfortune.

"I'll be damned. Knew she was a fighter, but she looks fit to take on the rest of you all!" Cyril boomed. It would've been a hell of a sight, but he was in no mood for delays. He fired, a crack marksman as ever with the bullet taking off a small piece of Siobhan's earlobe. She yelped out, clapping a hand to the wound, staggering back with a string of invectives. Esther rushed to her side, anguish plain upon her face.

Tobias cried out in dismay. "Don't hurt 'em or nobody else, sir! I'll tell ya, I promise!"

"That's mighty neighborly, son. Tobias, was it? Mountains are maybe half a day's walk from here and all of your folks are sure mighty comfy. What've you got there? Silver? Jewels? Nah, you tell me about the gold you got in them there mines. I already know everythin' from back in Independence."

"Yeah. Ya got it right. It's gold," Tobias admitted. He turned his head, not looking at Esther or Siobhan. "Nothin' like it anywhere else in the world! I'll lead ya there. To the mountains, sir."

"Call me Cyril, son. Lots of folks do. We'll take you up on that offer. Hell, I'll do you a solid and let the rest of your folk go even."

"Honest and true?" Tobias asked, his eyes wide with the same hope Cyril had seen a thousand times. The eyes of victims were mirrors, reflecting one another across an eternity.

"I give my word they walk free." Cyril gestured to the shivering survivors. It would take half a day to get to the mines and mountains, then another to get back. He would need to let the men rest after a job well done, but after that they would be easily capable of hunting down any survivors. Counting himself, there were still about twenty-five Blackhawks. "Trust me on that."

"I'll take ya there. To the mountains," Tobias said quickly. "I vow it on my mother's grave. I'll get ya what ya need, Cyril."

"Tobias!" Esther was pleading now. "Not the mountains. Ya can't!"

"The fella's got more sense than these fine ladies!" Cyril called, waving a finger at Esther. "You could do to learn somethin' from this here boy! Hope the nose is okay, Percy."

Percy only glared sullenly from above the hands clapped over his nose, red oozing between the fingers.

Cyril continued. "But it's evident he cares about you, Esther. Just to make sure he don't lead us in circles, the two of you are comin' with us."

There was no debate. The surviving townsfolk, weaponless and defenseless, would need to wander into the wilderness for what meager living they could scrounge up until the Blackhawks could return for their blood and souls. They looked to Tobias with a mixture of relief and sorrow.

Siobhan and Esther were led from the ring of survivors, prodded forth with guns in their backs. Weaponless or not, Cyril wanted them where he could have them monitored at all times. Siobhan was still clutching at her wounded ear, looking straight at Cyril. "Ya got no idea what you're in for in them mountains. Ya still have a chance to stop this."

Cyril raised his gun and shot a retreating man through the back of the head. "Each time you mouth off, I'll shoot another. That clear, girl?"

There were no further complaints about Cyril's final decision.

CHAPTER EIGHT

Lacey and Padraig had survived. The fires had not touched the stables. It was some relief for Esther as she led the horse out. The Blackhawks were watching from a distance away. Six men had their rifles trained on Esther and Siobhan, another two keeping them on Tobias. It was a multi-pronged threat to ensure they all remained in line. Siobhan felt Padraig's face, whispering endearments in Gaelic to calm him as Esther had seen her do a hundred times before.

"The mountains," Esther said grimly. She cast a gaze out in the directions of the Hungers, her breath quickening. Esther's heart pounded in her chest as a primordial fear blossomed there. "Tobias can't really be riskin' this."

"Mightn't be such a bad idea." Siobhan's voice bore more venom than a rattlesnake. "This's all his fault. Might as well let him take the bastards to the Hungers. Only downside's if they come after us."

Esther stopped saddling Lacey, delivering Siobhan a glare. The other woman was unable to meet her eyes.

"We ain't got all day, ladies!" Cyril shouted. He slung an arm around Tobias, tapping the revolver in his hand against the boy's shoulder. Even from the distance, Esther could see Tobias tense, trembling with Cyril holding him. He tried to pull away, but Cyril held him tight. "Let's all get a move on!"

Esther's words for Siobhan were soft. "Ya ever talk like that again, ya ever so much as hint that one of our people are expendable, I don't know there'll still be an us when you're done. My daddy's gone, Siobhan. He left this to me. And if it's only throwin' myself onto a sword so our folk can be safe, I'll do it. That boy's stupid and weak, but he's one of ours, and they would've come, anyways. I ain't gonna hear ya blame him like that."

Siobhan turned her eyes away, silent and refusing to admit fault. They'd argued before but had always managed to reconcile. Esther could never think of one of her people as expendable, not with so many already gone. Not with her father gone.

She tried without success to think of the last words Abraham had said to her. She found nothing, no inspiration she could draw upon. "Siobhan," Esther began, "I can tell them to leave ya here. Get clear, go off and find somethin' else. Find someone else. This is my responsibility."

"Ya ever talk to me like that again and you're damn right there won't be an us, Esther Foxman." Siobhan forced the smile, though her eyes beaded with wet salt. "Just stop talkin' like that. I love ya more than life, and if you're gonna walk into the Hungers, it's with me by your side. So shut up and stop givin' me an out." She took a shuddering breath, sounding like she was repressing a sob. She straightened up, setting her shoulders back.

"Let's go."

They led Lacey back to the group. Padraig followed with a whinny.

Cyril lifted an eyebrow. "Loyal boy, is he?" His hand tightened on the hilt of his revolver. He shrugged. "Tobias, just get on her horse. She and Esther are sharing the other."

Esther murmured an apology to Lacey as she finished with her saddle.

Cyril walked over, and she braced for another hit. "Hungry?" He offered her a strip of dried pork. "Wouldn't want you ladies starvin' now, little miss."

"Even if I ate pork, I don't eat with murderers." Esther displayed her Star of David proudly.

Cyril rolled his eyes. "Esther, everythin' you said earlier about Judas Maccabeus and Tecumseh was mighty dramatic and all, but you really should eat. How about you, Siobhan? I only winged you, shouldn't be more than a little sting. You hungry?"

A tiny chunk of Siobhan's left lobe was now missing, but she gave no sign she was in any pain from the wound, too busy glaring hatred at Cyril. She shook her head. "Not interested."

"Suit yourselves." Cyril shrugged. "I really must say, the two of you are handling this better than I thought you would."

Esther wanted again to ask if her lover was certain about the path they were taking. Siobhan left no room for doubt as they mounted Lacey together. Esther rubbed her horse's side as they set out, Tobias in the lead on Padraig.

The Blackhawks passed the time with idle chatter once they assured Esther and Siobhan would not be taking off in any sudden hurry. Cyril stretched languidly in his own saddle. "Tobias, lead the way."

"Yessir," Tobias answered quickly. Padraig obeyed his commands, trotting ahead with the mercenaries at his back. Esther kept her eyes forward, marching forth like a woman condemned.

CHAPTER NINE

They had passed the time riding in silence, heavy hooves tapping upon the ground as they kept to an even pace.

"You know, Esther, being with you is bringin' me back memories of the war when your daddy and I shared a trench or two," Cyril said suddenly. "He never ate no pork neither, did he, Percy?"

Beard only grumbled to himself, touching his tender, broken nose. His eyes darkened further when Siobhan tossed him an insolent grin. Cyril couldn't help but admire their tenacity and courage. Hell, he'd almost regret killing them when the time came, but there was no way he could risk having them on the loose.

"You got his spirit too," Cyril said.

"Expect me to take that as a compliment?" Esther threw back.

Cyril rolled his eyes. Try to be nice to folks and look where it got you. "Thought hearin' some stories might cheer you up a little. I might've mentioned before, but I really am sorry it went down like it did. Abe was a good soldier. I respected him in the past. Be a little less stubborn and the same won't happen to either of ya."

He had no idea if Esther believed him. Cyril suspected she was too smart for that.

When she finally spoke, her voice was soft. "We were livin' in peace," the girl said. "Not doin' harm to nobody.

Not the nearby towns, not any tribe on the plains. Why this, Redstone? Just for a little bit of money?"

"Ain't no rhyme or reason to it, girlie. Just old hungers come to call." Cyril dug his heels into the sides of his horse, spurring a faster trot as the mountains loomed closer. "It's how this nation works, how it was built. You had what people wanted and that was all there was to it. That's a hunger old as this here country, Esther. Long as there've been countries, there's been men like me, Percy, Nicky, and Bancroft. I'm a true, proper bastard, I admit. But the hunger in me is at least honest. It's the oldest hunger of all."

"Ya really think that?" Siobhan's lips curved upwards, a hidden knowledge lurking somewhere in her eyes, as though daring him to peer 'round a corner and ferret it out for himself. "Oldest hungers of all? Petty human greed?"

"It's petty, but it keeps me comfortable. Greed built this country. Greed's tamin' this country. Where you see grass and snow, there'll be iron and rail and smokestacks reachin' to the sky. People can get with that reality, or they can vanish."

"Ain't nearly the oldest hungers like you think." Esther's hand closed on Siobhan's, fingers linking as they squeezed. "My people've known worse than you through the centuries, Cyril, and they're still here in this land and in others."

"And which people might that be, Esther?" Cyril teased her. "The little Irish girl at least knows where she comes from. Which are you, Hebrew or Indian?"

"Who said I have to choose?" Esther asked. "I meant every word from before. I'm still here. Siobhan's here. Tobias is here. My people have fought, and they're never goin' to give up and die. You should know that."

"Well, sweetheart, I guess we can agree to disagree. If what Tobias there says about the gold in the Hungers here is true, me and my boys are about to be rich men. We'll be even wealthier when we clean up the town a touch and deliver the news back to the mining company." Cyril ripped at a piece of salted pork. "It really ain't nothin' personal, girl. It's just business."

The dark clay of the ground had given way to cold snow, each horse leaving behind a marking of its path as they sauntered forth into the mountain trails. Esther and Siobhan shivered, Cyril blinking away small flecks of white snow in his eyes while flicking his head toward the front. "Tobias! How far're we from your mine, lad?"

"Ain't far now. You can let Miss Esther and Miss Siobhan go now, can't ya?"

"See, I'd like to, my lad. But if I do that, you might get it into your head to do somethin' all stupid and heroic-like, which I confess would leave me real cross. It wouldn't help them one bit. All you'd achieve would be a pointless death that I'd make nice and slow for the inconvenience of it all. So I think it's best for all our sakes if you just keep on going. Right, Percy?"

Beard was glaring daggers at Siobhan, as if fantasizing about emptying his gun into her guts. But Siobhan and Esther, to Cyril's brief surprise, did not look frightened by him. Their eyes were not the eyes of frightened victims or defeated, broken women. There was determination there, even resignation. Theirs were the eyes of soldiers marching to the fight of their lives.

Tobias's voice was heavy as he called back. "It ain't much further now, sir. Maybe an hour at this pace!"

That was good, indeed. The horses would have time to rest and eat while Cyril and his boys took everything not embedded in the walls and ensured they might maximize their profits after burying the rest of their captives where nobody would ever find them.

The mountains towered around them, white-crusted tusks jutting up from a hungry landscape. Pure white and unsullied snows gave way for the incursion of horse and man as Cyril led the Blackhawks to their plunder. Something shifted above. Cyril saw movement in the crags of the mountain, dislodging powdery traces of snow before it vanished behind the peak. Mountain lions perhaps, maybe a goat. He didn't need to worry about such things attacking a contingent of armed men.

Cyril gave a shiver as a cold breeze scraped across the regiment. Some men hugged their coats around them tighter, Nicky downing his flask of whiskey quickly. "Hope that warms me up. It's too damn cold up here, Cyril."

"We won't be here long, Nicky," Cyril assured him. "Just think of when it's all done and we'll be some place nice and warm. Tobias, get us out of here quick, son. It's damn cold up here."

"I'm so sorry about this, Miss Esther," Tobias said, with no acknowledgment of Cyril's words.

"Just do what ya gotta do," Esther returned, her jaw set. "My daddy was brave to the end. We can do the same."

It was as though some secret message was passing between them, and Cyril did not care for that at all. Something else shifted above again, gone by the time he peered up. "Ya see any oddities there, Percy?"

"Hmm?" Percy stared at him, his nose raw and red from the earlier blow. "Sorry, Cyril, I was a thousand miles away. Ya lookin' for somethin' up there? Ya see the mine?"

Now that Cyril looked, the mountains were dotted by a series of dark punctures, many depressions all along the mountainsides that gave the impression of vast, frozen honeycombs. Cyril had ridden through every landscape known to man, but he had never seen anything like it. His hand tightened around the handle of his revolver, his eyes narrowing to slits. "Everyone, just keep close together." The terrain would be rough for horses soon. Too rough to ride them through the snows and rocks to the mines. "Ride as far as we can then we'll continue on foot. We'll leave a few boys behind and the horses can get some rest."

"Cyril … I don't like this." It was Ben's voice, soft and weak. "I really don't. We lost some good men back at Grey's Bluffs already. Maybe we can just get the payday. Go on back, that's all?"

"Shut the hell up, Ben," Cyril snapped. "Ya can stay back here with the horses if you're scared." No, there was nothing in this mountain worth fearing. Absolutely fucking nothing. He was Cyril Redstone and stupid ghost stories were just that: stories.

He reminded himself to watch the caves carefully. Unbidden, the stories of the Hungers came back to him, tales of people going missing. The longer he looked at the caves, the more logical that seemed. This place was a deathtrap. Anyone could have made a wrong step and fallen through one of those black holes. There were always logical explanations, no matter the superstition.

"Not worried about them running off?" Siobhan's hand closed tight around her lover's. "Things do have a way to get lost in these here mountains."

Cyril resisted the urge to shoot off her remaining earlobe, telling himself it was nothing but the whining keen of the condemned. His heart pounded with every step the horses took, the beasts of burden snorting wearily.

Nicky was downing another mouthful of whiskey, stating the obvious on everyone's mind. "We been ridin' these poor bastards all day, Cyril. They ain't gonna keep much longer."

"Right, I know." Cyril tried to urge his horse further, but the mount paused suddenly with a pitched whiny. It ground its hooves in the snow, all the horses stopping short. Above, Cyril thought he saw the trace of a shifting shadow by the mountains. Then it was gone a second later. He looked again, seeing nothing but a windswept peak.

He was just tired. He'd gotten no sleep with the raid and they'd been marching all day. Couple that with ghost stories, the cold, and bad terrain, you had a recipe for seeing things.

"Bobby, you take Garrett and Tommy." Cyril delivered his orders succinctly. "We'll leave the horses here. Let 'em eat, get some rest. We'll get in, take all the gold we can carry and get the hell outta here."

Something was wrong. Cyril felt it in his bones. Tobias seemed too eager to be helpful. Siobhan and Esther were a bit too defiant. The ladies were pale, shivering against the cold. But they were dressed warm enough, veterans at riding if the way they handled those reins was any indication. Living in the shadow of the mountains, they would be used to hard winters. Esther paid no attention to Cyril. Her gaze was instead directed at the mountains, her eyes scanning them intently. She murmured something to Siobhan in the tongue of her people that Cyril recognized but did not understand.

"English, ladies," he snapped back. "This here's America, after all."

He suddenly had the desire to turn back. But he was still surrounded by greedy men expecting more money for a day's work. He would have whatever treasure Grey's Bluffs was hiding here, claim as much from these mines as his hands could carry. He kept telling himself that, over and over.

Esther fixed her eyes on him, the snows pale against her tan face. "Ya goin' ahead, Cyril?"

He could not refuse and keep the respect of the men. Cyril dismounted his horse, boots heavy against the snows. He was suddenly enraged at himself. Why was he frightened? What was going on? Why was he letting himself be intimidated by this when there was gold to be claimed?

The metallic jangling of spurs against hard earth echoed about him, Esther shifting closer to Tobias and taking his shoulder in her hand. It was a gesture Cyril had seen before. The condemned liked to offer comfort to one another when they realized no mercy was forthcoming. Something, he realized, was *dreadfully* odd about this.

"Tobias," Esther murmured into his ear. "I need ya to know somethin'. It ain't your fault. It ain't. I don't blame ya."

"I hope I can make up for some of it, Miss Esther," Tobias whispered. "All those folks dead 'cause of me. It wasn't my choice to bring ya here."

"I know, Tobias. We were family there. All of us. *Khazak ve'ematz,* Tobias."

"What the fuck does that mean?" Cyril snarled, a sweat freezing on his brow. "I told ya before, English!"

"Dreadful sorry about that." Siobhan put a hand to her hip. If she was wounded, she wasn't acting like it. "It's just a phrase in Hebrew, means 'have courage.' I could say it in Gaelic if ya like."

"Just shut up. Keep your feet movin'." Cyril left the horses behind with his chosen men. He began to walk ahead, prodding his gun into Siobhan's back. "Walk."

She marched with the others, Tobias holding his head up high as he began to forge ahead on the mountain trails. Esther and Siobhan kept their hands clasped tightly, the Blackhawks murmuring and joking behind them. Nobody else seemed to notice anything amiss, as far as Cyril could tell.

They moved deeper through the mountain trail, through hard terrain, rocks and bladed peaks surrounding them. It was a damned labyrinth. How that boy knew where he was going, Cyril had no idea, but Tobias was taking them across with confidence and purpose. Even if there were mines, it seemed too far for anything to be reasonably extracted.

There was a rustle of wind, a strangled yelp. Cyril whirled with the dozen Blackhawks he had brought with him, all staring at the end of the procession. Cyril took a quick head count, realizing instantly that Lucky Bill Collins was no longer with them. A dark passage at the side of the mountain gaped from where he must have been standing.

"Stupid sonnuva bitch must've tripped. Fallen," Cyril mumbled. He looked into that dark mouth of the mountain, wondering if there was a drop, a loose stone by the entrance. He could see nothing from his position and did not care to stick his head in to find out. "More for us, right, boys?"

"Ya scared?" Siobhan's voice, her soft brogue tinged with little thorns of satisfaction. "There weren't no trip there. But ya already know, don't ya?"

"Shut your mouth."

"If only ya asked, Cyril. But men like ya never do."

Esther had stopped, facing him with a defiance in her eyes. "If ya hadn't killed my daddy and my people, we wouldn't be here now. Ya ain't ever comin' back for the others we left at Grey's Bluffs. I'd rather have not come here myself, but it's fuckin' worth it to ensure ya ain't makin' it out."

"What the hell are you talkin' about, you crazy little she-wolf?" Cyril could not keep his voice from rising in pitch, the men panicking all around him. There were whispers now, shadows sliding across the mountainsides. Not those of mountain lions or goats, but something else, for the shadows danced and slid across with the grace of serpents winding across the desert sands. They rose and Cyril could see them walking upright like men. Then they were gone again, fading into the blackness of the mountain openings.

"We know people like ya, Cyril. We've been dealin' with ya a long time." Esther leaned forward. The prospect of death and pain held no sway over this woman. One hand was in Siobhan's, the other locked around the star at her throat. "They been dealin' with ya longer. When we got here, we had to make deals, ya might say. They protected us if we wandered outta Grey's Bluffs."

Cyril thought of Mike Vinson, the man who had beaten Tobias, who had almost certainly planned something foolish. The man who had vanished in the night, his room drenched in blood.

Esther was smiling broadly. "Our land flourished if we left them alone. They didn't bother us. We didn't bother them. But now ya gone and brought a whole bunch of men with guns here. I think it's fair to say they feel *bothered.*"

Something landed in the snow before them. Cyril would have mistaken it for a heavy stone but for the sound it made on impact. The object rolled against the ground, leaving red stains in its wake. When Cyril looked closer, he recognized Lucky Bill's face, the mouth open in a silent scream. There were no longer any eyes, the dangling tail of a shattered spine hanging below a neck that had not been severed so much as torn and rent.

Cyril's mouth opened as the men screamed. He had to warn them they were giving away their location, that panic would do no good. Anything he was about to say was drowned out in the inhuman screech from one of the peaks. It was matched by an answering trill, a howl not unlike that of a wolf blended with that of a bat. Down the passage where Lucky Bill had vanished, Cyril saw a pair of torches blazing orange in the dark. No, not torches, he realized.

Eyes—something was watching them.

It was tall, slithering in the dark, body thick and strong. Silver knives pierced the shadows beneath those eyes, pressed together in a grimacing smile that would have made a bear blanche.

"I'm mighty sorry they wouldn't let me take 'em myself." Tobias sounded morose while men shrieked and raised their guns all about them. "Don't much mind if I live or die now, but it ain't right you're here, Miss Esther."

"Ya already apologized too much, Tobias." Esther sounded almost preternaturally calm. She said something in that other tongue again, holding even tighter to Siobhan. "It's okay. Seein' the look on his face is worth it."

Percival Beard tugged loose his gun, aiming it at Esther with a look of manic horror on his face. From the ledge above him, a pair of thick arms dotted with black and scarlet scales plunged down. Nails like thorns sank into Percy's eyes and his scream was like nothing human.

The arms jerked and dragged Percy up as he squealed and thrashed like a terrified pig all the while. The man vanished over the ledge, and the sounds of wet ripping began a moment later, coupled with a chorus of grunting satisfaction. The pig-squeals ceased shortly afterward, replaced by bones cracking and the splatter of organs.

Shapes emerged from the mountains. There were new shadows now, little orange lights burning in their faces as they descended towards the Blackhawks.

Esther lifted Siobhan's hand to her lips and kissed it. "Sorry you're here too, honey."

"Ain't no place I'd rather be than by your side, love. No matter what." Siobhan kissed her lips, the two acting as though they were in a moonlit grove instead of these cold mountains.

The men had their guns out, Cyril screaming for them not to fire, to wait until they had better odds, better shots. They didn't listen. Their discipline was washed away in a tide of terror. Three men were running from the main group, others standing to fire wildly at anything that looked like it might be coming closer.

"They're flesh and blood, dammit!" Cyril roared to his men. He was flailing now, lifting his revolver. "Wait'll you have a proper shot!"

He turned to see Esther and the others, his eyes blazing. His lips pulled back to reveal his teeth. "You. All your doin'!" He raised his gun in line with Esther's face.

Tobias was on him. Seizing his arm, the boy pulled, ruining Cyril's aim. Tobias sank his teeth into Cyril's skin and would not be dislodged, would not allow him to point the gun at Esther again.

"One of you idiots fuckin' shoot him!" Cyril shrieked. He punched Tobias in the ribs, his head, but the boy had a strength borne of madness. Then Cyril remembered he had the knife.

Pulling it free with his unoccupied hand, he brought it up and buried it in Tobias's stomach. The youth seized up and Cyril drew the blade upward with all his strength to open the boy's stomach. He ignored Esther's scream, felt the boy's grip slackening, and tossed Tobias aside.

The shadows landed before them. Cyril caught a glimpse of red and black flesh, of hard scales and white teeth. Too fast for his eyes to follow, they lunged forth, no bullets striking home. The men trying to flee were simply seized by large forms, pulled into the shadows of the caves.

Blood splashed against the snow. The air filled with shrieks of agony. One man tried to beg, his voice cut off as the shadow holding him buried its face in his throat, shaking like a dog with a bone as red splattered all about him.

Another Blackhawk raised his gun, but the twist of a shadow's arm left him with no gun and only a spurting stump where his hand had been a moment earlier. Silver nails flashed and white teeth snapped, cries of terror and pain extinguished. Replaced by the ripping of flesh and crack of bone.

The snow all around Cyril was red with the blood of his men. The Blackhawks were being rent asunder. Cyril had no idea how many men remained to him now.

He made to retreat when Esther hit him from behind.

***

Esther tackled Cyril with all she had, so hard that they almost hurtled down the peak. Cyril dug his heels stubbornly against the ground, trying to bring his revolver up. Esther seized his wrist, but he was strong, the desire to live overtaking him. She slammed her hand into the wound Tobias had given him. The gun sailed from Cyril's grip and clattered against the dirt road. Snarling like a cornered animal, The Blackhawks' leader drew his knife and stabbed behind him. Esther read each attack, shifting her body to dodge each one.

"Cyril, what do we do!?" one of the men yowled. There couldn't be more than six Blackhawks left, the creatures of the Hungers seeming to take their time to savor the remaining meal.

All Esther wanted was to keep Cyril from escaping, to assure he died with the rest of them. She could meet her father with a smile on her face then. Esther dodged a slash from Cyril's knife. The bastard was a lot faster than he looked. His eyes were those of a caged lion, desperate and feral. Esther evaded another attack, Cyril's movements lacking the finesse she remembered from Grey's Bluffs.

"Cyril!" A man's voice, wild and desperate, though Cyril paid it no heed. He sprang on Esther, stabbing down at her face. She caught his arm, shifting to turn this moment against him with a shove that sent him stumbling forward. Esther whirled to face him, seeing the carnage behind Cyril and what had become of his remaining followers.

The Blackhawks had formed a circle, a protective ring they no doubt hoped would see them survive. But the creatures of the Hungers did not attack. They paced about, growling in low, dulcet tones as if conversing among one another. The orange eyes were turned upon Esther and Cyril.

It was as if they were enjoying the spectacle.

Cyril recovered quickly, Esther realizing her distraction almost too late. She moved, not quick enough, the attack opening a red line on her shoulder. She reeled back, Cyril grinning in feral triumph as he prepared the next blow. Esther knew she couldn't dodge this time.

Siobhan hit him from the side, delivering a blow to his ribs that Esther swore she could hear. Cyril turned his attention to Esther's lover, slashing wildly. Forced back, Siobhan adopted a fighter's stance, her eyes flickering to the knife as she led Cyril on a dance. Cyril breathed raggedly, his movements slowing. He still had dizzying speed, but Siobhan was keeping ahead of the knife and delivering what punches she could.

Esther's gaze fell to Cyril's fallen revolver. She tensed to spring, when Cyril shrieked out a command: "Shoot her!"

The remaining Blackhawks raised rifles and revolvers alike. Esther lunged to seize the downed gun. With a swift motion, she rolled to her back and sat up, then lifted it and pulled the trigger. One man fell. He had a hole in his forehead, his brains spilling out the back onto the snowy trail.

The shadows roared in approval.

The other Blackhawks turned their guns on Esther, but panic left them sloppy. She dropped to one knee and took aim. She steadied her hand, remembering her father's lessons, and fired again. Her enemies' shots pounded the snows uselessly by her. But each of Esther's shots found her target. On the fourth shot, the revolver clicked empty, and she flung it from her.

The shadows converged on the remaining men, hauling them into darkness as they kicked and howled. Esther heard the sounds of ripping, feasting, followed by rumbles of satisfaction. She turned back in time to see Siobhan drive her fist into Cyril's nose, just as his knife caught her in the side. Siobhan cried out, dangling there like meat on a spit.

When Cyril made to pull it free, Siobhan grabbed his wrist, trapping the blade there. "Esther!"

Esther darted closer to the scene of the massacre, finding the nearest gun. She grabbed the dropped revolver after pulling it free from the severed hand holding it. She raised it and fired. Her aim was not perfect this time, but it blew a hole through Cyril's shoulder all the same.

***

Cyril heard the explosion, feeling a burst of pain at his shoulder. His arm went slack, agony exploding in his mind. Though he tried to order his body to obey, he could no longer move his dominant arm.

Then Siobhan dug her fingers into the wound and Cyril's world went white. All around, shadows of black and red with orange eyes tore his men apart with delighted snarls. Organs splattered to the grounds, the agonized shrieks of dying men mingled with the wicked snarls of these creatures. It sounded more like laughter than anything else.

Siobhan shoved Cyril, pulling the knife loose. Esther was at her lover's side right away, and they charged him together, their hands both on the knife.

It sank into Cyril Redstone's belly to the hilt, all fight leaving him at once. He stepped back, blood pouring from the wound as he gurgled out an empty threat. Cyril tried to raise his hands, to resist when vast shadows towered above them. He was pushed down, claws burying into his back. Cyril turned a pleading gaze up at the two women. They stared back with no trace of pity in their eyes. Thorns burrowed into his back, Cyril managing only the chirp of a trapped bird.

Siobhan clapped a hand to her wound, wincing as Esther held her. The shadows were about them, rumbling softly. They growled, and Esther faced them with no fear. "I'm Abraham Foxman's daughter. Ya know me. Ya protected me. I know we broke the deal. We know the conse—"

"That ain't true," the voice was a wheeze—*Tobias*, Cyril thought as he turned his head weakly.

The boy lay on the snow with a smile, not fear, plastered on his face as he spoke in a loud wheeze. "I led 'em here! This is all my fault. Esther and Siobhan were forced. These men wiped out Grey's Bluffs. I take full responsibility. It's on me."

"Tobias," Siobhan whispered. There were tears in her eyes now. "Nah, it weren't your fault. I'm sorry for what I said before. Ya don't have to—"

"I'm dead anyhow, Miss Siobhan. I ain't never been of much use. Might as well …" He laughed weakly, hand pressed against his wound. The laughter transformed into a moan. "Oh, God, it hurts … Just make it quick and painless as ya can, alright?"

A shadow knelt by Tobias. He closed his eyes, inhaling a deep breath as the burning lights gazed down upon him. The silver teeth hovered by his ear and the word it whispered chilled Cyril Redstone all the more for how human it sounded. *"Agreed."* It slipped a claw upon Tobias's head. Another went under his chin. Tobias smiled softly, his eyes closing. The thing's movements were oddly respectful. Gentle even.

Then the hands wrenched, and Tobias's neck broke with such force that pale bone protruded through the flesh. The thing that held him gently lowered the boy's body to the ground. His face bore a peaceful expression, as though Tobias did not know he was only meat now.

Esther and Siobhan had their eyes closed tight, tears pouring down their faces.

"Ya have your restitution now," Esther said resolutely.

"For what it is worth, in the memory of your father and your people, we will accept his life. No retribution to yours is forthcoming. What of this one?"

Cyril realized they were talking about him. He struggled like a worm on a hook, looking to Esther imploringly. "Esther. Esther, we can make a deal. I got more than you'll ever need. Just—"

"Like I said, Cyril," whispered Esther. She knelt beside him, looking him in the eye. There was no hint of mercy on her face. "There're older hungers. Men like ya figure they can take what they want. Ya think there's nothin' stronger than that. Ya spend your life driving out everythin' else. But there are things you've never dreamed of. They're still here, Cyril. They're still hungry." She turned to look at something over Cyril's shoulder, at what now dug its long nails into his ravaged skin. "We square? Ya left the horses alive back there when ya got the others?"

From behind Cyril came a primal voice, its breath reeking of an abattoir. *"We extend this mercy only this once. Do not return, Esther Foxman."*

"We're takin' Tobias's body with us. Bring it to a horse." Esther's voice was pure authority. It reminded Cyril of her father. The snarls echoed from around her, but Esther's eyes narrowed. "Ya weren't no good when we needed help. Ya can do this for me! He deserves a proper burial. Ya already got plenty enough to eat today."

Cyril felt such despair he could not even moan.

Esther and Siobhan spared not another look. Holding one another, they set off through the trail to leave the butchery behind them. The shadows parted to allow their departure. Only one followed, carrying Tobias's body.

Cyril tried to open his mouth, to negotiate and make some sort of deal, like Foxman would have. Then the shadows closed in, bringing their teeth and claws with them. Cyril Redstone understood some hungers were beyond all words.

CHAPTER TEN

Gerard Bancroft waited. It was not like Cyril to be late or uncommunicative. It had been nearly a week and a half since he had been dispatched to Grey's Bluffs with his merry band of cutthroats and there was still no word.

Perhaps Cyril had abandoned the job, Bancroft reflected as he returned home. Maybe the killer had turned sentimental after all. You could never tell when it came to mercenaries and soldiers. If that was the case, Bancroft would need to act quickly; Cyril knew far too much of his more illicit dealings to be allowed to roam free.

The miners and laborers were pacified and Independence belonged indisputably to him. Any remaining native tribes would be herded onto reservations to vanish. Bancroft & Hughes was the future. That could never be stopped.

Gerard Bancroft unlocked his door as he had countless times, locking it back up tight behind him. He lived alone now, having no care for anything but his business. His children were grown and seeing to their own endeavors throughout the territories. God willing, he would even see one become a senator one day. Governor. Maybe even higher.

He realized something was wrong the moment he reached his room. The window was open. It was then he felt the cold press of iron against the back of his neck.

"Sit down, Mr. Bancroft," the voice was low and hard, a woman's voice.

Bancroft froze as another individual crossed from behind him to close the window, drawing the curtains. He kept his voice level. "I keep little money in the household. There's a small safe. The combination is—"

"Not here for the money." The voice was biting now, and Bancroft recognized it.

"Esther Foxman," he said, immediately cursing himself for saying it aloud. He turned to see her there, the red-haired woman at her side. "Cyril betrayed me. Damn him." He sighed. "I understand you're upset, Miss Foxman. How much would it take to resolve this?"

"Soul of a goddamn banker," Esther muttered. She smiled, her voice brittle. "If it makes ya feel any better, Cyril didn't double-cross ya. The majority of Grey's Bluffs are dead. My father included."

"In that case I'll double what I was thinking of."

"Mr. Bancroft, some hungers can't be settled with money." Esther's voice was soft. "Sit down."

Bancroft's heart thundered against his breastbone, his throat suddenly dry. "Miss Foxman, if some misfortune befell your town, please rest assured that Bancroft & Hughes will give adequate recompense. I had nothing to do with any such violence as that was perpetrated by Cyril Redstone."

"Cyril's dead. He died screamin' if it means anything." Esther put an arm around the red-haired woman, squeezing her shoulder. "The funny thing is, it didn't really take much for folk in this town to give ya up, Bancroft. Somethin' concernin' popular folks talkin' about unions and wages who went missin' after Cyril came 'round. Turns out ya make enough enemies ..." She pulled the hammer back on the gun.

"You shoot me," Bancroft said softly, trying to conceal the fear he felt, "everyone will hear it. You will not be able to escape."

"Yeah, ya work late, so we had time to really talk about that. Work out the angles." Esther whipped him with the butt of her gun, striking his forehead. Bancroft fell back on the bed, dizzied from the blow and the starburst of pain that saw white dancing against his vision. "Siobhan, ya mind?"

"Not at all, darlin'." The redhead sounded satisfied, scooping up a pillow. "It ain't too fittin' for a great man like yourself, but it'll have to do."

Bancroft's eyes widened, and he tried to will his limbs to obey, but the blow had stunned him. The women had the pillow raised, lowering it onto his face. "They'll know … Hughes! My children will inherit the company! They'll know! Be reasonable! You kill me, the world'll be after you!"

"Bring 'em on," Esther Foxman said, just before the world went black in a soft and smothering embrace.

***

Tobias had been buried at Grey's Bluffs with the rest of their dead. It had taken a long time to dig enough graves for all of them. But Esther, Siobhan, and the remaining survivors, had committed themselves to the task and seen it through.

The bodies had been washed and then buried wearing white cloths and shrouds in pine boxes. Esther's clothes were torn. She had said the words her father had taught her with Siobhan and the rest. "Yitgadal v'yitkadash sh'mei raba b'alma di v'ra chir'utei; v'yamlich malchutei b'hayeichon u-v'yomeichon, uv'hayei d'chol beit yisrael, ba-agala u-vi-z'man kariv, v'imru …"

"Amen," they chorused as one. The horses were assembled, Lacey and Padraig awaiting their ladies.

Esther turned to the remaining people of Grey's Bluffs. "It ain't safe now," she said quietly, "for us all to be together anymore. Our town's gone, but we ain't." She took Siobhan's hand. "In my father's name … In Tobias's name. In the name of all we lost. We gotta love. There's enough money here for anyone to go and set up shop." She hated it. Time and again their people were killed, scattered and forced into diaspora and exile. "God willin', we'll meet again."

She saw their grateful eyes, the looks of sorrow as they departed, one by one, until only Siobhan was left with her. Esther fell into her arms, Siobhan holding her as she wept it all out—the fear, the pain, the guilt, and everything else.

Siobhan kissed her tears away, staying strong so Esther could permit herself some weakness. "I'm with ya, love. 'Til the end," she murmured. "The bitter end." She cupped Esther's chin. "Whatever anyone says, Esther Foxman. I love ya. From now come my dyin' day and an eternity after."

"I love ya, too." Esther kissed her back, tasting the sweetness of Siobhan's lips mingled with the salt of her own tears. There was little chance they could return to Independence now. The risk was too high. But they had money aplenty, and Esther knew Abraham had set up accounts just in case of a day like this. They might be hunted if any of Cyril's or Bancroft's associates could connect them to their disappearances.

She looked in the direction of the Hungers, picturing the creatures there. They had dwelled there since before there had been a United States, in their caves and their mountains. Theirs was an honest hunger. Not like that Esther knew they would encounter in the future. "The world's changin'. Cyril wasn't wrong about that. Not sure how long people like them can last, Siobhan."

"They lasted this long," Siobhan said. "But there's more out there."

Esther knew it was true. Abraham had known. Perhaps her mother had as well. She grasped tight to her Star of David and took a deeper breath. "I'm my mother's daughter. And my father's. I'm Esther Foxman. I'm Creek, and I'm a Jew. And I'm proud of both. And I'm yours, Siobhan. Long as you'll have me."

Their foreheads touched, their fingers interlinked, a soft substitute for an exchange of vows. Esther stepped back at last, walking with her lover toward their horses. "What now?"

"Ride in the direction of the sun," Siobhan said. "I figure we find the nearest town and see what's waitin' there for us. And we're together all the while. How's that sound?"

Esther smiled at her. That was it, when all else had failed. Her ancestors, her father and her mother's people had known it: victory was survival, when every single day was a triumph brought about by just seeing it. Her faith demanded that one did not accept the world as it was.

They had to try to make it better. There was only one answer to Siobhan's question.

"Like a life worth livin'," Esther said.

Then they were off, leaving Grey's Bluffs and the Hungers behind as life stretched out ahead of them on a road yet to be traveled.

About the Author

Zachary Rosenberg is a Jewish horror writer living in Florida. He crafts horrifying tales by night and by day he practices law, which is even more frightening. His forthcoming novel will be published by Darklit press and you may find his works released or forthcoming at Air & Nothingness Press, Nosetouch Press, and Seize the Press.

You may follow him on Twitter at @ZachRoseWriter

ACKNOWLEDGEMENTS

With writing as solitary as it is, I'm lucky to have the community I do. There are so many people I want to thank for this story and for giving me encouragement and support in writing it. I dedicate this to my parents Deborah and Nathan, along with my sister Julia for their repeated encouragement, and reminders not to give up.

My next acknowledgement is to Gabriel Kraan, one of the finest writing partners and greatest friends a person can have. Speaking of such friends, couldn't be here with the support of such incredible as Ai Jiang, Rae Knowles, Dana Vickerson, Patrick Barb, Elton Skelter, PL McMillan, Avra Margariti Christopher O'Halloran, Evelyn Freeling, Rebecca Cuthbert, Briana McGuckin and so many more. You all know who you are and I'm honored to know every single one of you.

I owe a special thanks to Taylor Rae for her patience, sensitivity, and answers to my many questions in putting together this story in this specific period. To Stephanie Ellis for her sharp eye and support, and to Sarah Chorn for helping change the way I think about writing. And of course, to Kenneth Cain, and Heather and Steve. Thank you for believing in this story and in me, and thank you for helping me polish it to the best it can absolutely be.

I'll see you all on the trails!

—Zach

CONTENT WARNINGS

Violence, antisemitism, war, torture.

MORE FROM BRIGIDS GATE PRESS

In an Old West overrun by monsters, a stoic gunslinger must embark on a dangerous quest to save her friends and stop a supernatural war.

Sharpshooter Melinda West, 29, has encountered more than her share of supernatural creatures after a monster infection killed her mother. Now, Melinda and her charismatic partner, Lance, offer their exterminating services to desperate towns, fighting everything from giant flying scorpions to psychic bugs. But when they accidentally release a demon, they must track a dangerous outlaw across treacherous lands and battle a menagerie of creatures—all before an army of soul-devouring monsters descend on Earth.

The Witcher meets Bonnie and Clyde in a re-imagined Old West full of diverse characters, desolate landscapes, and fast-paced adventure.

A family's relocation looked like a chance to relax and regroup—but as they settle into their new home, teenage Kimmie Barnes' special senses make her the target of something primordial, evil, and utterly malign.

Darkness ...

Golden Oaks, California is a sleepy town on the shores of Oro Lake, and the residents have no idea what horrors lurk below the glittering waters.

Beneath the waves ...

One by one, as people begin to disappear, the once quiet town is soon in the grips of a waking nightmare. An unimaginable horror consuming everything before it.

Hungry ...

All while echoes of an ancient evil spread out like malignant spider webs, like dead hands reaching, grasping ...

SEETHING ...

Who are we if not for the monsters that we keep?

They Hide: Short Stories to Tell in the Dark collects thirteen chilling tales that weave through the shadows, exploring the nature of fear, powerlessness, and control.

- A series of murders in a New England colony
- An untamed beast in pre-revolutionary France
- A mysterious stranger who invades 18th-century Ireland
- A traveling circus that takes more than the price of admission
- A gathering of the Dark, telling tales on the longest night of the year, and more.

Come play with vampires, werewolves, ghosts, zombies, ghouls and the devil himself. Make sure you check under the bed and don't turn out the lights.

Whether in an old weathered mine shaft, somewhere off the beaten path, out in the woods, or right here in the middle of this ghost town, danger awaits. We're going to take you way back, drop you right smack dab in the middle of the Old West at its finest. But we're not just going to give you shootouts and bullet wounds and blood splatter. Yes, those things are prominently featured, but there's so much more to this anthology of western horror.

Maybe it's a well-known creature popping in for a visit, or some new creepy crawly monster sucking out your soul, we're going to turn the Old West inside-out and explore its guts to the fullest. There are new adventures to be had, monsters both familiar and unfamiliar to be thwarted … And we're not always going to be the victors. Life in the Old West is hard, trying at its best, and it can wear you down quick.

So, prepare yourself to be transported back in time. Get yourself up on that rickety stagecoach, draw your guns, and let's get going. There's vast territory to cover here, and your journey begins now.

Featuring the talents of Antonia Rachel Ward, Nick Kolakowski, Villimey Mist & Damascus Mincemeyer, Jonathan Kemmerer-Scovner, Sean Eads & Joshua Viola, Craig E. Sawyer, Lana Elizabeth Gabris, Joel McKay, David Niall Wilson, Ej Sidle, Brennan LaFaro, Michael Bailey, Amanda J. Spedding, Taylor Rae, P.L. McMillan, Wen Wen Yang, Ben Monroe, and Chad Lutzke.

Visit our website at: www.brigidsgatepress.com

42169454R00075